# Alex & Anthony

## A HOOD LOVE TALE

# Jeneé

# PROLOGUE

*"You think I'm fucking stupid, don't you? You think I don't know you out here fucking everybody in the fuckin hood!" Mac shouted drunkenly across the dining room table.*

*"Mac, I don't even know what you're talking about, and I'm not going to do this with you in front of my daughter," Tika said calmly, trying to keep control of the situation.*

*"Your daughter? Aye bitch, that's my daughter. You ain't never been a fucking role model for her!" Mac shouted.*

*Alex jumped from the boom of her father's voice. She covered her ears to drown out the shouting as her parents continued their nightly ritual.*

*"Mac, please," Tika replied as the tears started to run down her face.*

*"Bitch, you do what the fuck I tell you to do, you hear me? You belong to me, I own you! Stop all that weak ass crying, too!" Mac spat, jumping up from the table.*

*Tika's fear of what her husband would do now that he was on his feet made her jump to her feet and grab Alex. She pushed Alex behind her for protection and the argument escalated.*

*"Alex, baby no matter what happens, you stay behind me, you hear me!" Tika shouted.*

*"Okay mommy," Alex cried out, now overrun with fear.*

*Mac lunged at Tika, backing her and Alex into a corner. He grabbed her by the hair and pushed her head into the wall. Alex was trapped behind her mother, forced to listen to the things that were going on over her head.*

*"Mac, please don't do this tonight," Tika begged, fighting hard to get away from him.*

*"Bitch, begging ain't going to save you! Shut the fuck up!" Mac spat, slapping Tika across the face hard.*

*Tika hit the floor with a loud thud. Blood gushed from her nose like a waterfall. Before she could get up, Mac started to stomp her where ever his foot landed. Alex sat there crying as she watched her father beat her mother, landing blow after blow leaving Tika to do nothing but cry out to him.*

*"Please Mac, I'm your wife and I love you. Please don't do this!" Tika cried out.*

*"Fuck you bitch, you ain't shit to me! You dead to me! You hear me, bitch!" Mac shouted, finally backing off of her.*

*Tika saw her chance to get away. She grabbed Alex*

*as she jumped up and ran towards the back bedroom that she and her husband shared. She closed and locked the door behind them, shoving Alex under the bed and going into the closet. Alex peeked from under the bed to see what her mother was doing. She could hear her father coming down the hallway.*

*Alex watched as Tika frantically looked through the closet, blood still pouring down her face. When she finally turned back around, she was holding a gun in her hand. She shook vigorously as she tried to load the gun before Mac could get in the room. He began to kick and pound at the bedroom door. Tika looked down at her daughter as tears streamed down both of their faces now. She reassured Alex that everything was going to be okay, knowing what she had to do.*

*Tika looked back up at the bedroom door as she pointed the gun and cocked it. When the door flew open, the rage that filled Mac's eyes terrified Tika even more. They stood there, Tika staring her husband down and Mac staring into the barrel of his gun. For a split second, it was like they were in a standoff, neither of them knowing what to do.*

*"You ain't going to shoot me, you scary ass bitch!"* *Mac shouted as he lunged at her.*

*Boom! ... Boom!*

5

Tika dropped the gun as her husband's lifeless body hit the floor. Rushing over to Alex and pulling her from under the bed, Tika ran out into the living room where she searched around frantically for a phone. Unfortunately, Mac started hiding the phones, so she didn't even know where one was. She walked over to her husband's body slowly, kicking him to make sure he was dead. She searched his pockets for his phone. When she found it, she dialed 911 immediately.

"911, what's your emergency?" The dispatcher answered.

"I shot my husband!" Tika screamed into the phone as the reality of her actions set in.

"I'm sorry ma'am, did you say you shot your husband?" The dispatcher asked.

"Yes, I couldn't get him to stop hitting me and I have my daughter here," Tika replied sobbing.

"Is your husband breathing ma'am?" The dispatcher asked.

"No, I don't think so," Tika answered, starting to cry.

"How many times did you shoot him?" The dispatcher asked typing in the background.

"Twice," Tika began sobbing harder.

"Okay ma'am, I am sending everyone out now," The dispatcher replied.

"Okay thank you," Tika ended the call.

She wrapped her arms around Alex as she replayed everything that had taken place as if it was happening all over again. It didn't take long for the sirens to be heard in the distance. Tika wrapped a blanket around Alex and they went out onto the front porch as the police pulled up in front of the house.

"Ma'am, do you or your daughter need medical attention?" A female officer asked as she walked up to the porch.

"I may, but I made sure he didn't hurt my baby," Tika replied looking over at Alex, who at this point, was in full-on shock clinging to her mother.

One officer escorted Tika to an Ambulance that pulled up shortly after the police arrived, another officer sat down next to Alex on the porch.

"Hey, there sweetheart," The officer said, trying to build trust between himself and Alex to see if he could get her to tell him what happened.

"Hi," Alex replied shyly hanging her head, not really wanting to talk to him.

"You don't have to be afraid anymore. No one will hurt you ever again. My name is Bear, what's yours?" He asked.

"Alex," She replied, finally looking up at him, more

*engaged in the conversation.*

*"Alex. That's a pretty name. Is it short for something, or is it just Alex?" Bear asked.*

*"It's short for Alexandra. Is my mommy going to jail for hurting daddy?" Alex asked innocently, worried for her mother.*

*"Well little Alex, your mommy did something big tonight and honestly, that would be something that is up to a judge, but I will make sure that you get taken care of," Bear replied.*

*"Okay." Alex smiled at him, as she started to feel safe around him.*

*Tika had received the medical attention that she needed. The police put her in handcuffs and in the back of the squad car. Tika's mother, Mary, pulled up to the scene running over to the car trying to talk to her daughter, but the other officers wouldn't let her close enough to it.*

*"Oh my god, my babies," Mary cried out as she took in the sight before her of her terrified granddaughter and her own daughter, all beat up in the back of a police car.*

*She ran over to Alex, scooping her up in her arms.*

*"Are you okay, baby girl?" Mary asked her granddaughter, wiping the tears from Alex's face as well as the ones that had started to stream down her own.*

*"I'm fine Nana, I just want mommy to come back,"*

*Alex said as the car her mother was in pulled off.*

*"Well baby girl, mommy has some stuff to take care of before she can come back, but you can come and stay with Nana for as long as you want," Her grandmother replied.*

*"Ma'am, are you a blood relative to this child?" Bear asked.*

*"This is my granddaughter," She replied.*

*"Okay. My name is officer Bear Pharr. Your granddaughter is going to be placed in your care until her mother's situation is figured out," Bear informed her.*

*"I can. Lord Jesus, help my baby!" She yelled, crying out to the heavens for her child.*

*"Okay, you know that you are going to have to stand before a judge before your guardianship can be legal and everything. We just need her with you for now. If you need anything, please don't hesitate to call me," Bear handed her his card.*

*"Okay, thank you, and you do everything you can for my baby. She was protecting herself and her child from that monster," Mary sobbed, hoping that everything would go well for her daughter.*

*"We will do everything we can ma'am."*

# Phase one

## While We're Young

### 8 Years later

# ALEX

The smell of breakfast pulled me from my sleep just as my grandmother tapped on my bedroom door. I sat up on the side of the bed and grabbed my cellphone from my nightstand, checking my notifications. After checking them, I stepped into my sweatpants and headed to the dining room.

"Good morning, Nana," I said after kissing her on the cheek and sitting down in the chair she kept in the kitchen.

"Good morning baby girl. How did you sleep?" She hugged and kissed me on the forehead.

"I actually got some good sleep finally."

"Well that's good. I've been praying and asking God to take those nightmares away from you," She replied with a small smile.

I hadn't really been in the mood to leave the house

lately. I had started to have nightmares about the night my mother killed my father, again. They disappeared for a while, but now they were back and in full effect.

"Thank you, Nana. It seems to be working well." My grin widened.

"So, you got any plans today?" She asked as she sat her fresh-squeezed orange juice on the table, smiling back at me.

"Well, Anthony and Bianca wanted to catch a matinee today but, I don't think I wanna be bothered anymore. It's my first real good night's sleep in a while. I just wanna stay home and relax," I sat down at the table.

"I always liked that Anthony. He is such a sweet boy," Nana gushed, pulling me out of my feelings.

"Nana, please don't do that." I was starting to become irritated.

"Do what?" She gave off a smirk as she walked back into the kitchen.

I honestly thought Anthony was really cute, and I could have been his girlfriend if the circumstances were different. It was just where I came from, your dude had to have fat pockets, or you were getting clowned. It was no-fucking-way I was going to do that to myself, so I had to play my role. On the real, though Anthony could get it, he was smart and funny, and he knew how to handle my fucked-up attitude. Nevertheless, I would never let those words come out of my mouth.

"You are so mean to him all the time," Nana continued to laugh.

"He is so lame, Nana. I could never see myself being with him. He's broke!" I whined.

Anthony was the first person to talk to me in the neighborhood. He was sitting on his porch one day when I was taking the trash out. I hoped that he didn't spot me on my way to the dumpster, but when I looked up at him, he locked eyes with me. When he stood up and started coming my way, I shook my head because I had put the idea in the atmosphere and couldn't be upset with anyone but myself. I was still dealing with my mother being gone, my life falling apart and learning to adapt to change, so I wasn't in a friendly mood.

*

*"Hey, you just moved in with Mary, right?"* He asked, sprinting to catch up to me.

*"Look, I don't want no friends okay,"* I replied with a slight eye roll, never breaking stride.

*"Dang, you mean ain't you?"* He asked sarcastically, chuckling as the words left his lips.

*"Look, I just fucking told you to leave me the fuck*

*alone. Keep fucking with me and I am going to stuff you in this fucking dumpster!" I snapped as I threw the bag in and made a beeline for the apartment.*

*Before I could make it back to the door of my new home, I looked back to see him staring at me from his porch once again. I rolled my eyes and walked into the house. The next day, he came and knocked on my door. I snatched the door open sucking my teeth.*

*"Look, I told you yesterday that I didn't want to be friends, so what do you want?" I snapped at him.*

*"Well, I didn't really want to be out here alone today and I kinda like your shitty attitude," he replied smiling.*

*I couldn't help but laugh at his honesty and once I showed him my teeth, he was hooked on me. For a week straight he came to my house trying to get me to come out and I would turn him down every time. School started shortly after I got with my grandmother, so of course, she put me in the school closest to the apartment. So, one afternoon while I was walking home from school, I could feel someone behind me, but I wouldn't turn around to see who it was.*

*"So, we live in the same projects and now we go to the same school and you still won't talk to me?" The voice asked.*

*I spun around, instantly knowing who it was.*

"Oh my god, why can't I shake you?" I spat, walking backwards.

"Seems like we crossed paths for a reason," Anthony said catching up to me.

"Is that what you think?" I asked dryly.

"Well, I think about a lot. For instance, I think that you are very beautiful, and I think that you are hurting from something," he replied genuinely looking over at me.

"Thanks, but you don't know shit about me, so stop acting like you do. We both know all you want is some ass. So, stop, please and thank you," I replied with nothing but attitude.

"Woah! I think you have the wrong idea about me. I am not like these other dudes out there. I really like you as a person; I'm not expecting anything from you." The scrunching of his brows let me know that he seemed offended.

"I hear that all the time in the hood."

"Well, I can show you better then I can tell you. That's if you let me of course." We slowed up as we made it to my apartment.

I looked at him for a moment to see if his body language would tell me something different, but all I got from him was authentic sincerity.

"Well, we can be friends, but you ain't my type, so

*that relationship shit is dead." I felt like I was creating boundary lines, but by the look on his face I could tell that he wasn't going to stop, but he respected what I was saying.*

*"That's cool, I will tone it down," he replied smiling.*

*I rolled my eyes at him, but on the inside, I was cracking up. I thought he was pretty dope and I kind of liked him too; that was my little secret, for me to know and nobody to ever find out. From that day on, Anthony and I looked out for each other and spent our days kicking the shit on my porch.*

*

"You think he's lame now, but soon he will grow into himself and I'm sure you will be singing a different tune," My grandmother replied, sitting a plate of pancakes and bacon in front of me bringing me back to reality.

"Nana," I said shaking my head and I jumped off into my food.

"Never say never, baby girl." She sat next to me at the table with her plate.

My grandmother and I laughed and talked until we finished our food. I helped her clear the breakfast mess, then it was time to really get my day started. I heard my phone ringing as I walked back into my bedroom, so I snatched it up.

"Hello," I answered while digging in my dresser for a clean pair of socks.

"Bitch, wake yo ass the fuck up!" Bianca's voice boomed through the phone.

"Bitch, I been up. What the fuck you want?" I shot at her jokingly.

"You still trying to catch a movie?" She asked. The phone went quiet as she waited for my response.

"Nah, I don't think I'm feeling all that today," I replied, now sitting on the side of my bed sliding socks onto my feet.

"Ol' homebody ass bitch. Well I'm about to come over there then," Bianca spat at me.

"Then why you still on my phone bitch?" I snapped, ended the call then tossed my phone on the bed.

Bianca moved into the projects about a year after I did. In the beginning, shit between us was rocky. She was one of those 'gotta be the cutest in the room', but she wasn't cute enough to be the cutest in the room kind of girls. She was hating on me at first, then one day I saw her getting bullied by some bitches outside of the liquor store. I wasn't the type of chick to sit back and let something like that happen.

I stepped in and held her down. Eventually, we started to grow on each other, and the rest was history. As time went on and we learned more about each other, we found that we had more in common then we knew.

It didn't take Bianca any time to get to my house since she only lived in the building across from mine, so when she busted into my bedroom I wasn't surprised.

"Bitch, did you see the shit Shawn put in the group chat?" She said as she closed my bedroom door behind her.

"Nah, I just finished breakfast." I didn't really give a fuck about what she was talking about, for real.

"Girl, he cutting up, he exposed Shay! Postin' all her nudes and everything," Bianca said.

"Damn, that's fucked up," I responded dryly.

"Why you so shitty?" She asked with her face turned up.

"I'm not shitty, I just don't give a fuck about that group chat shit. Especially when it's your ex exposing his current girl, who is actually your cousin. That shit is wack as fuck," I shot at her.

"Nah, bitch you just lame as fuck." Bianca laughed as she helped herself to my closet.

"But you at my house. Fuck outta here, and get yo bald head ass out my shit," I laughed too as I slid back on the bed.

"Bitch shut the fuck up because I can go home."

"Don't let the door hit you, bitch.".

Bianca was cool and everything, but I always felt like we were on two different ends of the totem pole. She was ratchet as fuck, always in some dude's face and in all the drama and I was more on the conservative side.

"Hoe, you will never put me out of nowhere," She replied laying back on my bed.

"You get on my fucking nerves bro," I said laughing as I repositioned my pillows.

"Anyway, so we not doing nothing today?" Bianca asked smacking her lips.

"I mean, I don't have no plans."

"So, bitch, if you ain't got no plans to put in place of the plans that you flaked out on, what the fuck is really going on?" She snapped.

"I'm just really not in the mood for all the random ass people," I replied sighing. Shit, I was being honest.

"Bitch you need to see somebody about that shit or yo ass goin be in the house for the rest of yo' fucking life."

"Yeah whateva." I hated when Bianca hit the nail on the head with her advice, but I knew that she cared for me and it was coming from the heart.

Once we got close, Bianca became the sister that I never had. We fought and argued a lot, but when it came time to have each other's back, I could honestly say that I trusted her with my life.

"Well, bitch can we at least get outside and see what we can see? I saw Kalel and them over at Ken's house," she hinted to me, smirking In the process.

"You gon' end up knocked up," I spat at her, still lying in the bed.

"Why would you say that?" Bianca sat up with a frown on her face.

"Cause, you always in a nigga's face," I snapped back at her.

Before the conversation could get deeper, my phone started ringing again. I looked down at the caller ID to see that it was Anthony.

"What's up?" I answered, hoping he didn't say anything stupid.

"Ya'll coming outside?" I could hear the urgency in his voice.

"Bianca was just talking about that," I told him as I finally sat up to find my shoes.

"What yall waiting on then?" Anthony snapped, now sounding like he was rushing.

"Boy fuck you. We will be out there when we get out there," I huffed, putting him on speaker.

"Well, Sanai out here talking cash money shit about

beating ya'll ass on sight."

"We on the way out." I ended the call.

Bianca heard the whole conversation so she was already out of the bedroom and damn near to the front door before I could put my shoes on. When Bianca flew out the front door, I was right on her tail.

"Bitch! You said what?" Bianca began cutting into Sanai before she was off the porch.

"Girl, fuck you!" Sanai spat, turning around to face Bianca.

I knew either way shit was going to end badly. I wanted to dead this shit before it became nothing more then a screaming match. Just as Bianca went to raise her hand to swing, I took Sanai's feet from under her. When I fell on top of her, I put my knees on her arms making it hard for her to defend herself, as I landed blow after blow right to her face.

The flood gates opened at the wrong time I knew I had way too much on my mind to be fighting. I took everything that I was feeling at that moment out on Sanai. I honestly think I blacked out on her ass because the next thing I remember is seeing the blood spewing from her nose, but I kept punching her.

"Talk yo shit na', bitch!" I could hear Bianca screaming from the sidelines.

My grandmother came running and screaming, just as

a police squad car pulled up. The officers hopped out with their guns drawn. I jumped off of Sanai and backed up to my grandmother with my hands up. Sanai was rolling on the ground screaming and holding her face.

"I need to see hands! Show me your fucking hands," One officer yelled while another went to check on Sanai.

"Y'all got any weapons?" The cop asked, walking up to us.

"No," We all replied in unison.

The officers put their weapons away once another squad car pulled up and they had a female officer check and clear us. By then, Sanai's mother had shown up.

"Lock that little bitch up! Who the fuck does she think she is?" Her mother shouted at the cops.

"Ma'am, this is a childish scuffle. Unless you want to be locked up for provoking a fight, I suggest you and your daughter go home," the cop told her. I could tell he wasn't in the mood for her shit. Fights like this happened every day in the hood.

"Fuck that! She needs to be fucked up like my daughter!" She screamed at the officer.

"First of all, bitch, you don't deal with the child, you deal with the adult. Now in order to get to her, you gotta go through me. Come on," My grandmother snapped gesturing for her to come over to her.

I guess it must have been the look on my grandmother's face that told her backing down was her best bet, because Sanai and her mother got the fuck on after that. The officers chuckled as they walked back to their cars, shaking their heads.

"What happened, Alex?" My grandmother asked, damn near snatching my arm off.

"She was talking crazy, so I nipped it in the bud." I shrugged uncaringly.

"Girl you are something else." Nana said laughing, patting me on the butt.

"Didn't I tell you to stay out of trouble?" Bear pointed at me as he walked up to Nana and me.

"Bear!" I yelped and then jumped into his arms. I hadn't even seen him pull up.

"Nah, you in big trouble young lady," he smiled, putting me back down on my feet.

"I was just defending myself." I was desperately trying to hold in my laugh.

Bear chuckled. "From the looks of things, I highly doubt that's what happened. She never stood a chance."

"She threatened me, so I beat her up. See? Just that simple

"Well you know just because someone makes a

threat, doesn't mean that you always have to respond. Luckily, these cops weren't actually here for this in particular, but next time, you might be going downtown, so you need to be careful with that hot head of yours." Bear pinched my cheek as he spoke.

Bear was like the father that I never had. He was always on Anthony, Bianca and me about keeping our grades up and doing as we are told. I fucked with Bear because I always felt like he understood life in the Martin Luther King projects. He saw how us young kids were surrounded by savages that had no real care about life and the things in it, be it theirs or someone else's.

Bear kept the promise he made to me the night I met him: any of my schooling needs or field trips that my grandmother couldn't afford, Bear was right there to take care of it. Anything my grandmother needed, he was only a phone call away. He showed me that there were still loving and caring people in the world and I loved him for that.

"You hear what he is saying to you Alex?" Nana chimed in.

"Yes Nana, I heard him," I replied quickly, trying to get my ass out of the hot seat.

"Okay, well I will be back through here a little later, I have something for you," Bear said, walking back to his

23

squad car.

"When you get back, it will be a hot meal waiting on you," My grandmother called out to him.

"Okay momma, I can't wait." Bear smiled as he got into his car.

The other cops retreated as well. My grandmother shuffled back into the house as the last car pulled off, leaving me on the porch with Anthony and Bianca.

"Damn baby, that shit was sexy as fuck," Anthony said to me, licking his lips and rubbing up against me.

"Boy, fuck you!" I snapped pushing him off.

"Damn, why you gotta act like that, baby?" Anthony rubbed my arm.

"If you touch me one more time, it's going to be a repeat of what you saw; only difference is, it's goin' be yo ass that's getting beat," I spat at him.

"You know I like that feisty shit," he replied, pulling his hand back.

"Anthony, get the fuck out my face bro." I laughed this time.

"Boy, why do you chase after a bitch that don't want you? You out here making yo' self look dumb as fuck," Bianca chimed in turning her nose up.

"You just mad cuz don't nobody want yo Booga wolf looking ass sir," Anthony shot back.

I busted out laughing. I couldn't believe that he cut into her like that.

I started instigating as I scrolled through my phone. "Flamed the shit out her ass, he on yo ass girl."

"Girl fuck you! Don't let me get on you and them crunchy ass white socks you got on," she shot at me, rolling her eyes.

"Aww Pookie, you mad now?" I asked sarcastically.

"Shut the fuck up talking to me Alex, like for real." I could tell that Bianca was starting to take things seriously.

I laughed at her again, amused by how she was now acting. "Don't get mad at me because Anthony cooked yo ugly ass."

"I can't even see how yall are still friends, all the fucking bickering yall do," Anthony said, sitting next to me on the porch.

"Real friends bicker." Bianca rolled her eyes.

"I will never understand women and their friendships. Y'all call each other bitches and hoes but will snatch other chicks wigs off for doing it," he laughed hysterically.

"Uh, because she is my friend and I can do that, da fuck!" Bianca snapped, rolling her eyes again.

"That is fucking stupid but, let a man do it and he ain't shit."

"Why are you so worried about what women be doing? You ain't getting one no time soon," Bianca spat told him sarcastically, laughing loudly.

"Bianca, you still mad that I don't want you?" Anthony asked with a straight face.

"Hell yeah," I butted in.

"Both of yall can kiss my ass," She snapped smacking her lips.

"Bianca, one day you will have someone that is just for you," I replied, looking over at her.

"It just won't be me, cuz Alex goin' be my wife. Ain't that right?" Anthony said, laughing and bumping my arm with his elbow.

I chuckled at his persistence. "Get over yourself."

We sat on the porch talking shit for a few more hours before Anthony and Bianca had to leave.

"Nana," I called out as I closed the door behind me. I could tell that she was in her zone in the kitchen because she had Bobby Womack serenading her through the record player she kept in the living room.

"In the kitchen." I could hear the pots and pans clacking together.

I walked into the kitchen, inspecting the two pots that were simmering on the stove.

"Aht Aht, get your dirty little hands out my food,"

She snapped, slapping my hand.

"My hands are not dirty, I haven't done anything," I replied, laughing and snatching my hands back.

"Don't backtalk me, little girl," She continued to throw down in the kitchen.

"Yes, ma'am." I smiled.

I decided it was best to stop while I was ahead, so I went into the living-room and turned the tv on. I searched through the tv guide, trying to find something worth watching until my phone started to buzz in my pocket.

As I searched the guide, I answered it. "Hello."

"Your voice is like an angel," I could hear the smile in Anthony's voice as he spoke through the phone.

"Boy, if you don't get!" I caught the profanity that almost flew out of my mouth.

"Man, you treat me so bad sometimes," Anthony replied.

"Don't be a pussy," I mumbled, so my Nana didn't hear me.

"Man, don't do me, bro," He replied laughing.

"Anthony, why are you on my phone?" I finally asked.

"Well, my uncle got me two tickets to the Pistons game this Saturday and I was hoping you could go with me."

"Oh, that sounds dope! Yeah I will go. What time would I need to be ready?" I asked.

"Well, my mom is taking me so, she said we should be walking out of the door at 8 p.m.," Anthony replied.

"Okay that sounds cool. Let me talk to my Nana and I will let you know if I can go," I told him.

I didn't find it odd that Anthony would ask me to the game, I couldn't lie and say that I wasn't nervous I had never been on a real date before. I was actually looking forward to seeing the game. Whatever happened after I would cross that bridge when I got there.

"Okay cool just hit me up later then," he replied.

"Iight," I ended the call.

I got up tossing the remote back on the couch and headed back into the kitchen.

"Nana, Anthony just called me and invited me to a Pistons game this Saturday. Is it okay if I go?" I asked.

"Who would be taking yall?" She immediately questioned, like I figured she would.

"Well, he said his mom was taking us."

"I guess I don't see anything wrong with that. My baby is going on her first date!" She shrieked happily.

"Nana, this is not a date. This is just two friends going to a basketball game," I was now becoming irritated.

I didn't really like talking about Anthony with my

Nana or any boy for that matter but that never stopped her from being her.

"That might be how you're looking at it, but I can guarantee that boy thinks this is a date, otherwise he would have invited someone else," Nana stated matter-of-factly while pulling her biscuits out of the oven.

I knew she was right. I knew how Anthony felt about me and I could see him using this as a ploy to get a date out of me. For a split second, I was a little smitten at his cleverness, but that quickly changed when I realized how fast I was to fall for it.

"Nana, please don't mess this up for me," I begged.

"I'm not trying to mess up anything, I am just teaching you how to read between the lines, so you don't go to this game thinking one thing and it's something else. Anthony adores you and you walk all over him." Nana continued to check on the food in the two pots that were still simmering on the stove.

"He is a guy, he can take it," I spat, trying not to look her in the face, scared that she would see how I really felt.

"Well you are going to keep right on until you look up and he is on to someone else." Nana gave a slight laugh and shook her head.

My grandmother's words made me slightly angry.

The thought of Anthony drooling over someone else bothered me for some strange reason, but I shook that shit off real quick.

"So, it's a yes, I can go?" I asked. I already knew the answer, but I needed an out and that was the only thing I could think of.

"Yes, baby girl, you can go," she replied.

I took the break in the conversation as my out. I didn't even go back in the living room, I went straight to my bedroom, pulling my phone out of my pocket and calling Anthony back.

"What's up wifey," he answered smoothly.

"Don't fucking play with me," I shot at him.

He laughed. "Go hard then, but nah what's up? What yo grandma say?"

"She said I could go, but she thinks it's a date," I told him, anticipating his response.

"I mean well it wasn't, but if you want it to be it can." There was no hint of hesitation in his tone.

Before I could rebuttal with some smart shit like always, Nana called my name, letting me know that dinner was ready.

"I'm 'bout to eat. I'll call you back, but I am going Saturday," I assured him.

"Tight, bet," Anthony ended the call.

I threw my phone on the bed and headed to the bathroom to wash my hands. By the time I got to the kitchen, my grandmother had already made my plate and sat it on the table. I sat down admiring the collard greens, mac and cheese, black-eyed peas, and the fried chicken that graced my plate. I blessed my food and began my feast. I was extra stuffed by the time I finished. I cleaned up my mess then went to take a shower. After sliding on my PJs, I flopped across my bed and grabbed my phone just to scroll a little on Facebook. Before I knew it, I had drifted off.

**Saturday**

"So, what time is your little date with Anthony?" I could hear the sarcasm and irritation in Bianca's question. The rolling of her eyes confirmed how she felt.

I knew that she felt some type of way about him asking me to the game instead of her, but she would never say it out loud. I knew her, and her vibe was all the way fucked up. Honestly, I found it funny that she talked so much shit about him checking for me and I wasn't giving him the time of day, but she was hanging onto his nuts like a pair of boxers.

"It's not a date bro. I am tired of people saying that." I huffed.

31

"You wouldn't be so mad if it wasn't true," she replied, sitting at the vanity straightening her hair.

"If you say so." I tried to find something to wear to the game.

"On some real shit Alex, why won't you give Anthony the time of day?" Bianca questioned, looking back at me through the vanity mirror.

"He's just not my type," I lied, trying to get off the topic.

"You a lying ass bitch, but whatever," she shot back at me.

"What you mean?" I now felt offended.

She replied candidly. "I know you like him, Alex. I don't see why you act like you don't."

"Girl fuck you," I shot at her.

"Whatever bitch! I'm 'bout to go over Ken's house and see what them niggas over there doing."

"Iight, I guess I will see you when I get back," I pulled my Nike jogging suit out of the closet, lying it across my bed.

"You got damn right. I want all the details," She told me as she walked out of my room, closing the door behind her.

I chuckled at her comment because I knew that she only wanted to see if I was going to give Anthony some ass. I kept trying to tell her that we were not the same when it came to the box. She passed hers out like it was party favors. Meanwhile, I was still a virgin. My grandmother snatched me from my thoughts when she poked her head in my bedroom.

"Hey baby girl," She cooed, smiling.

"Hey, Nana, what's up?" I asked walking over to get my underclothes from my dresser.

"Getting ready for your big date tonight?" She smiled harder.

"Nana," I groaned.

"I know, it's not a date I'm just messing with you."

"I finally figured out what I wanted to wear. I mean I don't really know how to dress for a basketball game," I admitted as I flopped down on the bed next to her.

"Don't overthink it baby, you're beautiful either way," Nana told me, pulling me in for a hug.

My grandmother could always tell when my anxiety was at an all-time high and she always knew what to say or do to bring me back down to reality.

"Thanks, Nana, I needed that," I kissed her on the cheek.

"Anytime baby."

She stood up patting me on the leg. Nana smiled at me again then grabbed my dirty close basket and went about her business.

***

The time had come for me to get ready for the game. I was convinced that time was in fast forward because it seemed like 7 p.m. came way faster then I expected it to. I pulled my hair up into a messy bun and got dressed. I debated with myself if I should wear makeup or not while I got dressed, finally concluding that a little concealer wouldn't hurt. So, once I felt that my outfit was good, I sat down at my vanity and applied my concealer. Just as I finished up, I heard the doorbell.

My stomach started to turn in knots. I couldn't for the life of me understand why I was so nervous. I had hung out with Anthony for over a year and being around him never made me feel this way. When I heard my grandmother call my name, I knew that I couldn't hide in my room any longer, so I grabbed my purse and headed out to the living room where I was met by my grandmother, Setra, Anthony's mother, and Anthony. When Anthony saw me, he couldn't even keep his mouth closed.

"Okay Alex, I see you," Setra said when I came around the corner.

"Thank you," I laughed.

"Yeah Alex, you looking real good." Anthony sized me up.

"Alright, y'all, let's get outta here. Y'all know this traffic going to be something else," Anthony's mother said as she pulled her keys out of her pocket.

I said my goodbyes to my grandmother and Anthony, his mother and I headed out to the basketball game. Anthony turned his gentleman up to a thousand by opening the car door for me and helping me into it. Setra chuckled at his gestures as he climbed in the front seat.

"Alex, how you been girl? Keeping them grades up?" She asked as she pulled out of the projects.

"My grandmother wouldn't have it any other way," I replied, snapping my seat belt.

"I know that's right. I wish you could rub off on your homeboy up here," She nudged Anthony's arm while laughing.

"Ma, please don't embarrass me." Anthony hung his head.

"Embarrass you? Boy, you betta stop while you ahead," She shot at him.

I admired Anthony and his mother's relationship. Somehow, they had found the perfect blend of parent and child relationship and best friends, and it worked for them. Most times I tried to not be around for my friends' family moments because it brought back too much for me to handle.

"So, Alex how are you feeling about going to the 10<sup>th</sup> grade?" Setra asked.

"I mean, it is what it is I guess," I answered honestly.

"Well, you just keep up the good work and don't ever let anything stop you because without education, this world will eat you up and spit you out." Setra spoke as she fiddled with the radio.

I sat back taking in everything that she was saying. I knew that her words held hella truth and I made a mental note to hold onto the gems of knowledge that she was dropping on me. Before long, we were pulling up in front of The Little Caesars Arena. I had never really gotten the chance to experience Downtown Detroit. I couldn't lie, it was dope as fuck being in the heart of my city and seeing how much life it had and how well it was thriving.

"Okay, ya'll. Have fun and call me if you need me," Setra told us, handing Anthony the tickets as he got out of the truck. He opened my door and reached out for me to grab his hand so he could help me out.

"Iight ma, I got you," Anthony replied closing my door behind him.

We walked in and the security guard sent us through the metal detector, then the usher checked out our tickets and pointed us in the direction of our seats. As we walked to our seats, I could feel Anthony looking over at me.

"What the fuck are you looking at?" I snapped looking at him crazily.

"I can't admire your beauty?" He smiled at me.

"You are a fucking weirdo," I told him, laughing.

We finally made it to our seats, and I was amazed at how close we were to the floor.

"Yo' uncle sell drugs or something?" I asked.

Anthony held a smirk on his face at my question. "Umm, not that I know of, why do you ask?"

"I mean what nigga you know giving seats like this away?"

"It was actually a late birthday present," Anthony replied, clearing up my confusion.

The announcer came on and the lights went down as the game began. Anthony and I got comfortable in our seats, ready to enjoy the game. I knew absolutely nothing about basketball, but I was glad that I agreed to come because basketball was actually dope. I laughed at the way Anthony screamed at the players when they made bad moves. I caught myself staring at him, watching how comfortable he was and how he was just being himself. It was like I was seeing him for the first time.

Even though I was sixteen and Anthony was only a year older than me, I still wasn't that deep into boys. I mean don't get me wrong, I found guys attractive, I was just so fucked up on the inside that I created a hard exterior so that no one would even attempt to get that close to me. Anthony knew what to do to get me to drop that wall. After screaming and hollering at the player for a while, he finally sat back down.

"You mad or nah?" I asked sarcastically as I sipped on my slush that I had gotten from the vendor walking through the crowd.

"Basketball is a big thing for me," he laughed.

"Clearly," I laughed as well.

"That slushie looking real good," Anthony said, implying that he wanted me to share.

I put my cup back in the cup holder that was in the arm of my seat. "Boy, fuck you! I don't know where your lips been."

"I love that feisty ass attitude you got man. That shit sexy as fuck to me." Anthony gave me a look he had never given me before.

It was at that moment that the dynamic changed between me and him. It was like something sparked inside of me from the look he gave me. I started to feel something I had never felt before. Like any other time, I hide my feelings and just tried to get through the rest of the game and get back to the house before my wall crumbled.

When the game was over, Anthony called his mother to come pick us up. It didn't take her long to get to us and before I knew it, we were back in the projects. Setra parked her truck by her building and told Anthony to walk me home. I was starting to feel like Setra, and my grandmother were in cahoots to get me and Anthony together.

He got out of the truck and opened my door as he had done before we left, helping me out of the truck once again. We began to walk to my apartment.

"I really appreciate you coming out with me tonight," Anthony said, breaking the silence.

"I appreciate you asking me to go." I tried not to blush.

"Well, you knew I wasn't taking Bianca's crazy ass and you know I don't fuck with none of these dope boy ass niggas." Anthony rubbed his hands together.

"Yeah that would have been something to see with her ratchet ass.".

"Alex, can I ask you something?" He asked as we walked up to my porch.

"What's up?"

"What is it about me that makes you not like me?" he stared at me, waiting for a response to the question.

I decided to be real with him and myself. "I am just

fucked up and I don't want to mess someone else up spilling my shit out on them."

"Well, my mother always tells me if someone is really down for you, they will have your back, flaws and all. So even if we never make it to some relationship shit, just know I always got your back." Anthony finally understood that I was dealing with my own demons.

"That's the dopiest shit anyone has ever said to me," I admitted, blushing.

"Glad to be the first to do it. It's late. Try to get some rest. I know my mom is going to be calling for me soon."

"Okay, good night. See you tomorrow," I turned to walk up onto the porch.

As I passed by him, he leaned in and kissed me on the cheek, then took off running. I was stunned because he had definitely caught me off guard. I snatched the door open, making a beeline for my bedroom, reeling from what had just taken place. I passed by my grandmother who was peacefully sleeping in the recliner in front of the tv.

When I got into my room, I took off my clothes, put my pajamas back on and climbed into my bed. I laid there thinking about how soft Anthony's lips were on my cheek and how sweet he really was. I could feel myself starting to fall for him. I knew things between us would be different, but I still couldn't see myself being his girlfriend.

# ANTHONY

My mother and I moved into the Martin Luther King projects about a year after my father died from a long battle with lung cancer. She had gone into a deep depression and the bills started to back up as money started to become scarce. I would never forget the day the Landlord and the Sheriff's came and put all of our stuff out on the curb and told us that we had to leave the only home that I had ever known. We house hopped for a short while, then one day my mother got a phone call and she came running to me telling me that we were moving.

I was excited but I damn sure wasn't going to say that I wasn't a little worried about someone coming to put us out of this house, too. When I saw the new place that I was to call home, I wasn't so sure about how I would adapt to the new environment. Everywhere we looked a nigga was slinging something. My mother made it very clear to me that she was not having that shit from the moment we walked into our new apartment. Getting an education and making something of my life was a big thing for my mother. She always told me she didn't want to see me make the same mistakes that she had made.

I watched her work two jobs to take care of me and

41

all the bills on her own. I always told myself that one day, I would be well enough off to make sure that she never had to work another day in her life. In the meantime, I made it my business to keep my grades up in school and learn everything I could.

I was getting ready to go into the 11th grade when I met Alex. She had just moved in with her grandmother. Of course, living in the projects, everyone gossiped so I knew a little about her story before I actually saw her. My mother told me that one of the neighbors told her that Alex's mother killed her father protecting her, and that she had been put in jail. Alex would be moving in with her grandmother Mary for a while. My mother encouraged me to reach out to her because she would probably need a friend, and my mother and Ms. Mary had gotten close and she figured that Alex would be nothing like the other girls.

About a week later, I saw her for the first time. She was taking out the trash. My mother had also given me information that she was about my age, so I was expecting to see some frumpy chick that was still growing into her body. Imagine my face when I saw her and how mature and stacked she was. I just knew I had to shoot my shot. I got up and headed over to the dumpster to talk to her. At first, she was mean as fuck, but I could tell that it was just a wall that she had put up to protect herself. From the things that I had heard about her and her home life with her mother, I could understand why she would feel like she needed to guard herself.

I kept up my persistence until we came to a common ground with the way that we felt about each other. I knew that Alex was the girl for me, but she had made it up in her mind that I wasn't the guy for her. From then on, we decided to be close friends after I kissed her one night. I can't lie and say that I wasn't fucked up about being put in the friendzone when I just knew I had gotten her for sure. We continued talking our shit and chilling like before, but as we went into a new year of high school, I could feel that things were different between us and I started to see less and less of her. It got to a point the I would see her leaving and then I wouldn't see her come back for days to weeks. Everyone was looking for her. Alex's grandmother was starting to get really sick and she was nowhere around to take care of her, so I would go and take out her trash while my mother would cook for her.

One day I was coming out with the trash and I saw Kalel's truck pull up. She and Bianca jumped out laughing, walking up to the porch.

"What the fuck are you doing?" Alex spat at me.

"Taking out your grandmother's trash," I answered,

confused at the way she was coming at me.

"Damn nigga, you couldn't get Alex so you going for her grandmother?" Bianca spoke and Alex busted out laughing.

"Nah. Shit, Alex wasn't here so somebody had to do it," I snapped at them, instantly killing the laughter.

I could tell by the look on Alex's face that she knew I was on her ass.

"Boy fuck you," She pushed past me and went into the apartment.

Bianca stood there looking at me stupid as hell.

"What the fuck are you looking at?" I snapped at her as I walked off the porch to the dumpster.

I heard her suck her teeth as I walked past. Bianca and I had a real love-hate relationship. She was one of the often-left unsupervised fast ass girls my mother talked about like a dog. I watched her as she chased after Kalel and his homeboys as they had their way with her, and I told myself that I would never touch that, even with gloves on. So, when she told me she was feeling me, I had to tell her the truth. Of course, she didn't take it all that well, but we were able to be cool. I started to notice a change in her too, but I was the type to peep shit and just move accordingly. Shit was starting to get out of hand.

I tossed the bag into the dumpster, cussing to myself.

I couldn't believe Alex was letting Bianca get in her head and get her caught up in the bullshit. As I walked back past the apartment, Alex came back outside with a small duffle bag.

"This you now?" I asked as she came down the porch.

"When did you become my daddy?" She snapped at me, scrunching up her face.

"Nah, I ain't trying to be that at all. I'm just trying to figure out where my friend went. This ain't you Alex, and you know it."

"You ain't her daddy, ol' bitch ass nigga! Come on Alex. Fuck this bum ass nigga. He can't do shit for you anyway," Bianca butted in, grabbing her arm and pulling her towards the truck that they had gotten out of.

Alex walked away looking back at me with a glance in her eyes that I had never seen on her face before. I knew there was nothing that I could do to change her mind, so I just walked back to my house, shaking my head as the truck pulled off. Apparently, my mother could see that something was bothering me when I walked back into the house.

"Is Ms. Mary okay?" She asked with a concerned look on her face.

"Yeah. I took out her trash and I made sure she was eating the plate you sent over before I left out," I told her as I sat down in the dining room.

"So, why is your face all turned up?" Ma asked, looking through the cabinets trying to figure out what she was going to cook.

"Nothing important," I answered dryly.

She looked over at me. "It's important enough for you to be wearing it like a coat."

My mother knew me like the back of her hand, and I knew that I couldn't lie to her about anything, so I just gave in.

"Alex came back while I was taking the trash out."

The look on my mother's face changed from concerned to annoyed instantly. It caught me off guard because I had always known my mother to love Alex.

"Why that face?" I asked.

"I just don't like the person she is letting that fast ass Bianca turn her into," she admitted with her words drowning in her emotions.

"The feeling is mutual," I told her honestly.

"Well baby, you can lead a horse to water, but you can't make it drink," she walked over and rubbed my arm.

"I just thought she was different. I thought that night after the game that I was in there." I hung my head.

Ma chuckled. "That was your first mistake. You can't assume with women."

"I know, I just wanted her so bad Ma," I replied like any young boy who was watching his childhood crush turn into a person that he never knew she would turn out to be.

"Baby, this is all a part of life. Everyone that you think is supposed to be here an eternity is not always meant for an eternity. Like my mother always told me, you wanna hear God laugh, tell him what you have planned."

"I guess you're right, Ma," I replied exhaling.

"Well, on a lighter note, I'm making gumbo and sweet potato muffins for dinner, your favorite," she smiled softly.

I knew that she had only come to that decision in a plot to make me feel better. I really wasn't in the mood to eat anything, but I didn't want to break her hurt turning down her efforts.

"I can't wait," I feigned happiness.

"Got get some rest. I will call you when it's ready," She replied, walking over to me and putting her arm around me to pull me in for a hug.

"Yeah." I stood up from the table.

I kissed my mother on the cheek and headed to my bedroom. I pulled my phone out scrolling through my call log until I came across Sage's number. I hit the call button and put the phone to my ear as I flopped across my bed.

"Hey, you," Sage cooed into the phone.

"What's up? You sound like you're having a good day," I said, smiling into the phone.

"It's a day. My mom forced me to go to the grocery store with her," she replied with a sigh.

"Well, you have to learn at some point. What you goin' do when ya man get hungry?" I asked sarcastically.

"My man? When did I get one of those?" She shot back.

"I was just saying."

"So, what do I owe the pleasure of this phone call Anthony?" She asked, cutting into me.

"Just wanted to hear your voice," I replied telling only half of the truth.

"And?" She asked. She must have been able to hear the bullshit in my voice.

I met Sage maybe six months earlier. She transferred to our school from some high school down south when she moved into the projects with her aunt after her mother was killed in a car crash. We clicked instantly; she was easy to talk to, she made me laugh and we could spend hours together and just chill. I could see myself being with Sage, the only problem was her uncle never liked me for whatever reason. He would snap every time he found out that I had been with Sage or I had been talking to her. One time he sent her brothers to come jump me so that I would stay away. I did, but only because Sage begged me to. She told me that her uncle was a very powerful man and he would hurt me if I didn't listen to him.

I didn't want anything to happen to my mother or myself, so we decided that we would only talk on the phone and at certain times of the day. Eventually, feelings started to form but we never acted on them because we knew it could never go anywhere. I always felt like if it was meant then it would be, but over time, Sage became a good friend that I was able to confide in.

"I just got a little bit of shit on my mind." I finally gave in to my need to vent.

"I'm listening. You know I don't have a lot of time," Sage replied.

"I saw Alex today," I said.

"How did that go?" Sage knew how things had gotten between Alex and me from previous conversations.

"She is turning into a completely different person," I said exhaling.

"Everyone transitions through life differently," Sage replied calmly.

"I mean I get that, but you don't shit on the people that hold you down," I repositioned myself in the bed.

"Anthony, I know how you feel about that girl, but you can't keep chasing her. She is a little girl lost, and you ain't Supaman."

I fucked with Sage's realness. She was never one to tell me what I wanted to hear, which let me know even more that her care for me was genuine.

"Yeah, all I can do is let it be," I replied trying to convince myself that I could let it go.

"So, on a lighter note, how is your mother?" She asked.

"She's smooth, still crazy as ever but she smooth."

"Don't do her," Sage laughed.

We talked for a few hours and the conversation was just starting to get deep when I heard a noise in her background, then I heard her gasp.

"Oh shit, I gotta go," She whispered, ending the call.

I closed my eyes and prayed that she was able to delete my number from her call log, because if not, shit was about to get real bad for me. I heard my mother calling my name as she came to my bedroom door to tell me that dinner was ready. I tossed my phone on the bed and got up opening the door just as she was about to knock.

"Dang, you hungry now, huh?" Ma asked while laughing.

"I guess you could say that," I replied, sliding past her

to get to the kitchen to get some food.

Even though I was trying really hard to enjoy my gumbo with my mother and clear my head, I still couldn't stop thinking of the look on Alex's face like she wanted to stand up for herself, but she felt like she couldn't. All I could do was keep helping my mother take care of Ms. Mary and hope that Alex came around and got her shit together.

"Let God handle it, baby," I heard my mother say, pulling me from my thoughts.

"I know ma."

*** 

A couple of days later, Alex still hadn't been back, and I had not seen her at school. I hadn't seen much of Bianca either, so I knew the rumors of them ditching and going with Kalel and his boys were true. I got closer to the apartments as I walked home from school. Something about the air said something wasn't right. I stopped at Ms. Mary's to check on her as I did every day. The moment I opened the door, the smell hit me hard.

I covered my nose and walked deeper into the apartment calling out to her but getting no response. When I got to her bedroom door, I jumped back at the sight before me. She was sitting up in the bed with her head back and her mouth wide open.

"Ms. Mary!" I called out.

She didn't respond.

I ran out of the apartment to mine to get my mother. She jumped up from the couch when I came busting through the front door.

"Ma! Ms. Mary! She's not moving!" I shouted breathing heavily.

"Call 911 Anthony!" She shouted back, putting her house shoes on.

The look on my mother's face revealed all the fear that she felt. she ran past me out of the door. I dropped my backpack and pulled out my phone. I hit the emergency call button and put the phone to my ear.

"911, What's the emergency?" The dispatcher sounded almost robotic coming through the phone.

"Uh, yes I have an elderly woman that is not responding," I replied, my voice shaking.

"Is she breathing?" She asked.

"I don't think so, please hurry," I pleaded, now pacing back and forth on the porch.

"Okay, I am sending everyone out now," She replied.

"Okay, thank you," I said ending the call.

I could hear my mother screaming from across the street. I shoved my phone back in my pocket and started running to her. By this time, the neighbors had started to come out of their apartments, probably to inquire what had my mother screaming like that. When I got back to Ms. Mary's, I found my mother on her knees on the side of the bed, holding Ms. Mary's hand.

"Help is coming Ma," I sat next to her and wrapped my arm across her shoulders.

I pulled my phone out again and called Alex. She didn't answer the first time, as usual. We didn't talk much anymore so I assumed she didn't see it important enough to answer for me anymore. I called her a second time and she answered on the first ring.

"Hello." There was straight attitude seeping from her voice.

"Alex, you need to come home," I said, tears starting to run down my face.

"What the fuck are you talking about Anthony!" She snapped.

In a soft tone, I told her again. "It's your grandmother, you need to come home."

I didn't want to tell her the ins and outs over the phone. I was sure that she would have wanted to come home and say her goodbyes to her grandmother in person. I could hear the sirens getting closer to the projects.

"Are those sirens?" Alex asked, starting to panic.

"Come home Alex!" I shouted.

"I'm on my way," she said, right before the call ended.

I threw my phone down on the floor next to me as I broke down watching my mother break down. The next thing I knew, the paramedics were coming into the apartment.

"Ma'am, are you a relative to this woman?" A female EMT asked my mother.

"No, but she was like a mother to me," she replied sobbing.

"I'm sorry, I am going to have to ask you to step outside and give me and my partner room to work," The EMT replied.

I got up and helped my mother to her feet as we did as we were asked and let them do what they needed to do. I lead her back over to our apartment because people had started to crowd around, and I knew how my mother was about people seeing her vulnerable. Once she was as comfortable as she could be and had everything that she needed, I went back out to make sure that everything was alright.

Just as I was getting back across the street, I could see Kalel's truck in the parking lot. As I got closer to Ms. Mary's apartment, I could see that there was no one in it. Then, I heard the most blood-curdling scream; one worse than my mother's. I rushed into the apartment, catching her just before she hit the ground. Kalel rushed over and snatched her out of my arms.

"Fuck you think this is, nigga! Don't touch my girl again!" He snapped lifting Alex up to support her better.

I looked up at him in shock. His girl? I couldn't believe a word he was saying. Alex would have never fallen for a nigga like Kalel. I could see the hurt forming in Bianca's face. She had always had a crush on Kalel, and I knew that she would have never been cool with them hanging around each other if she knew that he really wanted Alex. She ran out of the apartment, making a beeline for her own. I backed out of the apartment, still in shock and headed back home to check on my mother.

When I walked in and saw her sitting on the couch, a bottle of Jack Daniels sitting on the table in front of her. I already knew what type of night it was going to be. I hadn't seen my mother drink like that since my father died. I kissed her on the forehead and went to my bedroom, closed the door behind me and laid across the bed. After a few hours of staring at the ceiling, I began to drift off and none of the events of the day mattered anymore.

# ALEX

It had been about two weeks since my grandmother's passing. Bear came and helped me with all the arrangements and her funeral was coming fast. I had heard about the stunt that Kalel pulled on Anthony after I passed out. I knew that Bianca was hurt because I hadn't talked to her since that day, and when I called her phone, it went straight to voicemail, so I figured I was blocked. I was super pissed the fuck off at Kalel for the way he outed us, but I was glad that it *was* finally out. I was tired of playing a role.

I had been spending my days smoking weed and staring at my grandmother's bedroom door. I hadn't been eating or sleeping. Hell, I rarely came out of the apartment after everything that took place. I wasn't ready to deal with everyone and their fake love and pity. I knew I would have to deal with that bullshit at the funeral. To be honest, the only person I really wanted to deal with wouldn't even look at me.

I knew that Anthony was upset about the news of Kalel and I being together, but I had to do what was best for me and my life. Besides, Kalel was good to me. He took care of all my needs. He gave me money to take care of things when my grandmother first started getting sick. I would go to parties with him and be his accessory and he would throw money at me. I took that as my way to make shit right for my grandmother and myself. Now with her being gone, I was going to need Kalel more than ever. The month was almost over, and the project manager knew that my grandmother was gone so I only had so much time left before I was going to be in the streets.

I was alone and in a bad headspace, I was just about to light another blunt when there was a knock at the door. At first, I was going to answer, but something told me that it wouldn't have been a good idea. Ignoring my gut feeling, I walked over to the door anyway and slowly tugged it open without looking to see who it was.

"Can I help you?" I snapped.

As soon as I made eye contact with the person on the other side of the door, I knew I fucked up, and bad.

"You must be Alex. I'm Samantha from the Department of Child Services. Can I come in and talk to you?" She said in a bubbly tone.

"I would rather not. You can't say what you have to say from out there?" I snapped at her repositioning myself at the door so she couldn't see into the apartment.

"I guess I can work on your terms, for now. I know that you have been through a lot of in the last couple of weeks and I'm new. However, due to the fact that you are not

16 yet, you cannot be emancipated and released out on your own. So, because Setra promised me that she would look after you for the next few days, after your grandmother's funeral if no one steps up to be your legal guardian, you will be placed into foster care. Then, we will work on my terms." She spoke with a slight hint of attitude.

Samantha had been around the projects for a while taking people's kids and breaking up families, so just about everyone knew who she was in the hood.

"Girl, fuck you!" I snapped, slamming the door in her face and locking it, going back to the couch and lighting my blunt.

Foster care was the last place that I wanted to be. I had met girls all over the projects that had been in foster care and the stories they told would scare the boogeyman. I had to come up with a plan and fast. I knew that no one was going to step up for me. I pulled out my phone and called the only person I knew would have my back.

"What's up, Queen?" Kalel said answering the phone.

"Hey love, can you come to scoop me up? I need some air," I replied.

"Iight baby, let me shoot this move real quick and I will." He replied. I could hear him talking to someone in the background.

"Iight baby, just hit me up when you get close. I'm

'bout to jump in the shower," I replied putting my blunt out and standing up.

"Wear something sexy. I'm taking you out tonight," Kalel replied before hanging up.

I had no idea what I was going to put together that even equaled sexy. My grandmother had always let me get myself together, but if it was too tight or too short, it was absolutely a no for Mary. I stood there looking at my grandmother's bedroom door, wondering if there was something in her closet that could have helped me at this moment. I hadn't opened it since the day she was found, and I couldn't lie; standing there even thinking about opening it was scaring the shit out of me.

I walked closer to the door and reached out for the handle, I paused taking a deep breath. I pushed the door open and closed my eyes, pep-talking myself to open them. When I opened my eyes, everything just started playing back like it was happening all over again. I saw everyone there and it felt so real. I grabbed the knob and slammed the door shut. I was just going to have to make do with my clothes.

I took a quick shower and went into my closet to see what I could find. After tearing up my bedroom, I decided on a cute mustard colored long sleeve bodysuit and a pair of skinny jeans. I dug through the bottom of my closet and pulled out my black knee-high boots. I sat down at my vanity and put on a little concealer. I was giving myself a final check when my phone started to buzz on my dresser. I looked to see it was a text from Kalel, letting me know that he was outside. I jumped up and grabbed my jacket and bounced out of the door.

The sun blinded me as I walked to Kalel's truck. My eyes had to adjust since I hadn't been out in so long. I put my hand up to cover my eyes. The moment Kalel saw me, he started cheesing hard as fuck.

"Damn girl," He said looking me up and down.

"You like it, daddy?" I asked in a sexy tone.

"Fuck like it, I love it," He replied pulling out of the projects.

"So, where are we going?" I asked checking myself out in the mirror in the visor over my head.

"It's a surprise, sit back and ride, you know I got you, baby," Kalel replied with a sexy grin.

I giggled as I sat back in the seat doing as I was told. Dave East blared from the speakers as we pulled up to our destination. It was a ratty-looking building with no writing on it and it was painted all black. At first, I was a little nervous, but when the door flung open and I caught a glance inside as we passed by to turn around, I became interested to see what was going on.

We parked and got out of the car. When we walked up to the door, Kalel pounded three times and after a few seconds, the door opened up and we walked in. Security patted up down and we began to move through what I had figured out was some sort of clubhouse. Kalel was slapping fives with different people as we walked through until we finally made it to the bar.

The bartender's face lit up when she turned around and saw Kalel standing there.

"What's up handsome," She said over the music.

"What's up baby girl. Let me get two rum and coke on the rocks," Kalel said leaning into the bar so she could hear him.

The bartender bounced away to fill our order. Kalel turned around and looked at me, giving me the same look that he was giving me in the car. The bartender came back with our drinks interrupting our moment.

"Here you go, and you know that is always on the house baby," she said smiling.

"Thanks, boo," Kalel said winking at her as we walked away.

I followed him deeper into the club. We finally came to a small set of steps that lead up to a little area with a few couches and a stripper pole. Kalel whispered something in the security guard's ear, and he stepped aside, letting us in. I found a section in the corner where the light was a little dimmer so I could check out the spot and see what was going on around me. To my left, there were a few bitches on the dance floor twerking on each other. To my right was all the fellas at the bar trying to talk to the wallflowers that were standing nearby.

Kalel pulled a microphone out of his bag and turned it on.

"What's good? It's ya boy, Killa K in dis bitch! How yall feeling tonight?" He said, hyping up the party.

I was impressed because the whole time that I had known him, I had always seen him as a regular-ass dope boy. I would have never thought that he was a party promoter as well. I watched on as he got the crowd hype as fuck. I noticed that people kept coming up to him slapping him five, but it wasn't until I actually watched what was going on.

The people would come into the club, go to the bar and place their orders. The bartender would throw up a sign with her hand. If Kalel had what that person wanted, he would nod his head and they would come over to him and make their transaction. If he didn't have it, he would point across the room to another nigga that also had a microphone and the customer would go over to him.

I had to admit, the set-up was clutch as fuck, but

nothing this good would last forever, so I knew I had to watch my back when I was with him. There were still niggas in the streets that went for their target and they didn't care who was with them when they hit, either. In between hyping the crowd and mingling, he would come back and check on me.

"Hey, you got plans for the rest of the night?" Kalel asked, coming close to me, so he didn't have to yell.

"Nah, not for real," I replied, curious to why he was asking.

"We having an after-party at another venue, you wanna go?"

"Yeah!" I was glad that I didn't have to go right back to the apartment.

"Okay, we leave here at 2 am," He walked away and got back on the mic.

I sat there, bobbing my head to the music. After a little time, the little private area started to get a few more people. This chick came and sat next to me. She sat her purse, which looked like a fucking body bag, up on her lap and pulled out a sack of weed. I watched on as she pulled out a pack of Backwoods and began rolling the fattest blunt I had ever seen in my life. She sealed it up and ran the lighter across it to dry it off.

She finally lit it and took a long drag off of it and then passed it to me. I was caught off guard because where I was from, you didn't share your weed unless it was like a close family member or something. I took the blunt and took a long drag, exhaling and hitting it again before passing it back to her. We talked and laughed. She kept rolling blunt after blunt, and the DJ was in the pocket like a muthafucka with the playlist that he was running.

Before I knew it, Kalel was coming to get me telling me it was time to go. When we got to the next venue, I noticed very quickly that the atmosphere changed and in a major way. When we walked in, the first thing I noticed was a good portion of the people in the club were completely naked. Just like before, Kalel walked through slapping people five like he knew everyone. I followed behind him in awe. We came to another closed-off area with a stripper pole. When I got comfortable, shortly after a small group of people came in as well.

Kalel and the people in the group happily greeted each other as if it had been a long time since they had seen one another.

"What's good baby!" The guy with the long beard said loudly, slapping Kalel another five and hugging him.

"What's good my nigga," Kalel replied smiling.

"You know me, you ready to take this trip?" The man

asked.

"Been ready," Kalel replied.

The man pulled his necklace off and twisted the top off exposing a little spoon with a small mound of white powder on it. Kalel took the spoon and put it to his nose, snorting the contents right on up. I knew drugs were real, I had just never seen them face to face. My mother never did drugs and all my father did was drink, so I had never had that placed before me. I was interested. I wanted to know what it would feel like to be high, and no one was here to stop me.

I was grown and on my own now that my grandmother was gone. I made my own choices.

"You wanna take a trip too, baby girl?" The guy with the beard asked with a creepy smile.

"Uh...sure, why not," I replied, just wanting a moment to escape from everything that was going on in my life.

He dipped the little spoon inside of the necklace again and I repeated what I had seen Kalel do. My brain felt like it was going to explode. Everything became so intense. My pussy was running like water and I was ready to party. I got up and started dancing to the music that was playing in the club. Looking over the half wall, I could see the rest of the club, realizing that people were actually having sex.

I'm talking hardcore fucking, the shit that I had only seen on the videos that Bianca used to sneak from her momma's stash. The music started to fade as the DJ changed gears and you could hear people moaning loudly and crying out. I turned to tell Kalel what I saw. He was stroking his rock-hard manhood staring at me like I was a piece of meat, like somebody had hit the 'fuck me' switch, turning everybody into sex slaves. I had never done anything like this, so I stood there high as hell, sheepishly not knowing what to do.

"Come here, I will show you what to do," Kalel gestured for me to come to him as he bit his lip.

I walked over to him hesitantly, sitting next to him on the little couch. He took my hand and put it on his dick in place of his own and started moving it up and down in a stroking motion. I followed his example and began stroking him on my own.

"Yeah baby, just like that," Kalel moaned, laying his head back.

His words made me stroke faster as I started to give in to the lust that had built up inside me from the drugs.

"Oh, shit. Don't' stop Alex, you goin' make me buss!" Kalel whined, repositioning his feet.

I kept my rhythm going as my heart rate started to pick up. I could tell that something was about to happen from the way that his legs were shaking, but before he could get to his grand finale, he jumped up and flipped me over on all fours. He reached around me, undoing my belt just as the guy with the beard came back in with his necklace out once again.

"I see it's getting hot in here, yall want another bump for the road?" He asked smiling.

"You know I am always game," Kalel said, smacking me on the ass as he stepped over and got his next fix.

"For you, little momma?" The guy asked.

Before I could answer Kalel butted in.

"Yeah, she goin need it for what I am about to do to her," Kalel replied laughing, slapping me on the ass again.

On some honest shit, Kalel's comment made me nervous, but I knew to chicken out was not going to go over well, so I leaned over and snorted the contents on the spoon. This time, everything started moving in slow motion and I didn't even feel like myself anymore. Kalel snatched at my belt until he got it undone. The aggression that he had when he pulled me out of my pants turned me on even more.

He stepped back and admired my ass as he rubbed and kissed on it. By this point, it was sticking straight up in the air. I watched him as he walked over to a little cabinet in the wall, something I would have never noticed if he wouldn't have opened it. He pulled out a bottle with a clear substance in it. He walked back over to me and began pouring what I quickly figured out was oil, all over my ass and legs.

"Damn girl. You just as sexy with your clothes off." He rubbed the oil into my ass, slapping it every now and then.

I was on autopilot by now. The drug had taken complete control of my body, so when Kalel rammed himself into my ass, I didn't even flinch. I could feel my body starting to warm up like he had hit a button inside of me.

"Oh shit," I cried out, grabbing onto the couch.

"Yeah, you like that don't you bitch," Kalel pushed deeper into me.

"Yes daddy, don't stop," I whined.

The voice that came out of my mouth scared me because I had never heard it before. I almost couldn't believe that it was coming from my mouth. I continued to cry and moan as Kalel popped my anal cherry.

"I'm cummin!" I cried out involuntarily.

Before I could actually grasp what was going on, my body exploded. I could feel my juices running down my legs.

"Damn girl, yo shit wet as hell," Kalel said, pulling out and pulling his pants up with a wide smile on his face.

I dropped on my stomach on the couch, trying to

catch my breath. I had never so much as masturbated let alone busted a nut, so my body was trippin, and I was sure that the cocaine in my system did its part as well. I looked over at Kalel and I remembered seeing him laughing then he leaned down, so we were eye level.

"Congratulations, you passed the test." He slapped my ass and then walked out of the private area. I reached for him, but I couldn't move, The next thing I knew, I was out.

When I opened my eyes, the room was bright. I sat up and looked around, realizing I was in my bed and Kalel was nowhere around. I had no idea how I got back to the projects. My clothes were in a ball on the floor and my cell phone was sitting on the little table next to my bed. I grabbed it, looking at the time. It was still early morning, so when I heard a knock at the door, I was confused at who it could be.

I got up and threw on one of my long t-shirts before running to the door. I opened the door thinking it was Kalel, but I was face to face with Bianca. I pushed the screen door open and walked over to the couch. She came in, closing the door behind her.

"Hey," She said walking over to the couch.

"Hey," I replied dryly, wondering what it could have been that she wanted. I hadn't talked to her in some time and I had come to grips with that fact that weren't friends anymore.

"Look, I know that we haven't talked in a long time, but you are my girl and I don't fuck with these otha bitches the way I fuck with you," She blurted out.

"You stopped talking to me," I told her while lighting the piece of blunt that I had left in the ashtray.

She looked at me and turned her face up.

"When you start smoking weed like this?" She sat down in the chair next to me.

"When did it become your business?" I snapped at her, taking a long drag off the blunt.

"Look I didn't come over here for your shitty attitude, okay! I came to apologize to my friend," She snapped at me shifting in her chair.

"Apologize? For what? Leaving me when I needed you most over a nigga that never liked you from the beginning?" I shouted, feeling the pain all over again.

"Alex, you're right and I'm so sorry. Your grandmother's funeral is tomorrow, and I didn't want this weighing on you on such a big day," Bianca said, wringing her hands.

"You really think this shit is important enough for me to be thinking about it while I lay my grandmother to rest? The only reason you over here kissing my ass is cause you and your raggedy-ass momma need a ride to the funeral, and you know I got them fucking family cars. I would put the whole Detroit Zoo in my shit before I did anything for you or yo' fucking momma! Girl fuck you! Get the fuck out my house!" I replied jumping up from the couch throwing the blunt in the ashtray and walking over to the door.

I snatched the door open and stood there, waiting for her to leave. She stood up from the chair with the dumbest look on her face and stormed out of the door. She turned around to say some slick shit and I slammed the door in her face. I understood that Bianca liked Kalel and all, but I had always thought that our friendship outweighed any nigga, and when I realized that wasn't the case, I knew how I had to deal with her.

I went back into my bedroom, grabbing my phone up to call Kalel and tell him what Bianca had just done, when I noticed a text from Anthony.

*Anthony: Hey, I am sure that I am the last person that you want to hear from, but I was just checking on you. I hadn't heard from you since everything happened with your grandmother...*

I kept reading the message over and over wanting to call him, but I decided against it. I knew how Kalel felt about that and I was with him now, so I wanted to keep shit right with him. I closed out the message and went back to my original plan and called Kalel.

"Good morning party animal," He said chuckling.

"Shut up. How did I get back here?" I asked, still confused about my action towards the end of the night.

"Well after the club we went and got some food from the Coney. When we got back to your house, you were still riled up, so we fucked some more and then when you passed out I put your food in the fridge and rolled out," He replied candidly.

"Oh my god, I don't remember any of that." I was ashamed of myself.

"Well, I do, and that shit was dope as fuck. You nasty as fuck by the way. I love that shit." I could hear him smiling.

"Shut up, don't make me feel worse than I already do," I said laughing, not really feeling bad at all.

"Never feel bad for being you," Kalel shot at me.

"Any who, let me tell you what I actually called to tell you," I said, changing the subject.

"What's that?"

"Guess who came knocking on my door this morning," I said waiting for him to guess.

"Let me guess. That weak ass nigga Anthony," Kalel snapped. I could hear the irritation in his voice just from saying Anthony's name.

"Nah, ya girl," I smiled.

"Bianca rat ass? The fuck she want?" He asked.

"She came over here talking about she's sorry and she wanted to apologize so that this bullshit with our friendship wouldn't be weighing on me while I was trying to lay my grandmother to rest." I busted out laughing.

"What fucking tip do she be on?" Kalel shot back laughing himself.

"I have no idea. I told that bitch I knew she was only talking that shit because she and her raggedy ass momma needed a fucking ride to the funeral," I said, getting irritated all over again.

"I hope you told that bitch to go find a bridge to jump off of."

"I put that bitch out of my house!"

"That's my baby. These hoes get no mercy," Kalel replied, adding fuel to the fire.

"Yeah, I wasn't for her shit at all. Like, you leave me when I need you most over a nigga and then come back after not saying one word to me or even checking on me for that matter, and I am just supposed to welcome you back with open arms? Hell nah, I ain't that bitch," I snapped.

"Don't let that bitch pull you out your square. I need you to have a clear head for tonight," Kalel replied, instantly taking my mind off of Bianca.

I raised my brow. "What's happening tonight?".

"Got a job for you," he replied.

"So that means I'm going to make some money?"

"Big money, if you play ya cards right," He replied chuckling.

There was another knock on the door. At first I ignored it, but the knocking wouldn't stop. I ended my phone call and stormed out of my room to the door, snatching it open.

"What the fuck do you want," I snapped.

"You to watch your mouth," Bear replied, moving me aside and walking in the apartment, sitting on the couch.

"My bad Bear, people just been getting on my nerves." I wiped my forehead, closed the door behind me and walked over to the couch.

"What's going on with you lately?" He said, cutting to the point of his visit.

"What do you mean?" I asked confused.

"I been stopping by and checking on things and I noticed you getting in Kalel's truck. Are you fucking with him?" Bear spat at me.

"Why is it any of your business who I'm fucking, Bear?"

"I want you to be safe out here. I told your

grandmother that I would look after you," he replied, changing his tone and repositioning on the couch.

I rolled my eyes. "My grandmother is gone. She is not coming back. I am not your responsibility; I can take care of myself."

"What has you so angry? I'm just trying to look out for you," Bear spoke with a concerned look on his face.

"Look out for me? Where were you when the bitch from child services came knocking at the door to tell me that if no one steps up to take me, that I will be going into foster care? So, you goin take me in, Bear? Huh! You going to take me in?" I started to cry.

"Alex, if I could, I absolutely would. Right now, I don't think the way that I am living would be right for a teenage girl," He hung his head.

"See, that's the shit I'm talking about right there. Everyone wants to tell me what I should do, or they keep telling me that they want to look out for me, but nobody is stepping up when I need to be looked out for, but Kalel! So, don't come in here asking me who I am fucking and what I'm doing with my time unless you plan on doing something to change it," I snapped, my chest heaving up and down at this point.

Bear just sat there looking at me. He was speechless

for the first time since I met him. I waited a few more seconds for him to say something, but he never said anything.

"Just get out," I said, finally breaking the silence.

He looked at me and sighed as he stood up from the couch and started walking towards the door.

"I wish you nothing but the best," He spoke over his shoulder as he walked out the door, closing it behind him.

I flopped down on the couch instantly regretting everything that happened. It was just too much on me and I didn't know how to handle it. I sat staring at my phone, thinking about the fact that I had no one to call. I opened up my contacts and tapped Anthony's number and was getting ready to call him when my mind got the better of me and I closed it out. I finally snapped out of my feelings, tossed my phone on the couch next to me and got up in search of my purse.

I found it tangled in my jeans from the night before. I grabbed it, looking for the sack of weed that Kalel had given me a couple of days before and the last blunt wrap that I had. I found the weed that I was looking for, but as I dropped the purse back on the bed, a little baggie fell out and the contents caught my eyes instantly. I turned and looked to make sure that I was seeing what I thought I was seeing.

A little baggie of powder laying on my bed. As soon as my brain registered what was going on, my mouth started to water. I looked at the bag of weed in my hand and back at the bag of cocaine on my bed for a few seconds, then I snatched the baggie up and continued on to the living room. I sat down on the couch and poured a little of it in my blunt wrap, then I sprinkled a little powder on the weed and wrapped the blunt.

I sat there for a moment, looking at the blunt on the table and I thought back to how good I felt the night before. The way all my problems just seemed to melt away when the powder entered my system. I grabbed the blunt and lit it, taking a long drag from it, feeling the euphoria of the drug mixture entering my bloodstream.

I laid back on the couch, enjoying my high and listening to my thoughts. I smoked and smoked until I was so high that I couldn't even lift my hand anymore. When I finally got the energy to move, I put the blunt in the ashtray and got up to take a shower. I got myself cleaned up and dressed and went and checked my phone again. Just as I was about to put it back on the couch, it started to buzz in my hand.

"Hey baby," I said, seeing Kalel's name on the caller ID.

"Hey beautiful, you ready for some fun?" Kalel asked in a giddy tone.

"I am. You ready to tell me what we're doing?"

"I told you, I got a job for you to do," he replied. I knew he wasn't going to tell me, so it made no sense to keep asking. I just moved on with the conversation.

"What time are you coming and what should I wear?" I asked smacking my lips.

"I'll be there in about 10 minutes, and don't worry about clothes. I got all that set up for you," he replied his background was starting to get loud.

"Okay I will see you then," I said, ending the call before I even heard what he said.

I was geeked about the fact that I was going to be making my own money. I knew the kind of money that Kalel made and If I was able to network with his connects, I knew I could make just as much, if not more. I ran to my vanity to make sure that I was looking good and put together like I knew daddy would like me to be. After a short while, I started getting antsy and I found myself pacing as I waited on Kalel to pull up.

I sat back down on the couch and grabbing my blunt and lit it again. I took one long drag off of it and put it out, mellowing instantly. I wasn't sure how long I was out of it, but the next thing I remember was Kalel blowing his horn. I grabbed my jacket and my purse, shoved the weed and the cocaine baggie in my purse and headed out of the door. I jumped up in the truck and kissed Kalel on the cheek and we were on our way.

I watched on as the road turned from paved to dirt. I knew we weren't in Detroit anymore.

"Where are we going?" I asked shifting uncomfortably in the seat. I was becoming nervous.

"Why? You nervous?" Kalel asked laughing at my demeanor.

"Nah, I just wanna know where you taking me," I was starting to get a little irritated.

"Well, you know I wouldn't let anything happen to you," he replied, looking over at me for reassurance.

"I'm sure," I replied dryly.

Kalel chuckled as he drove on not saying anything else. We drove down the dark dirt road for a little while longer before pulling up to what looked like a little shack. He parked his truck and jumped out, leaving me lagging behind. I grabbed my shit and jumped out behind him. I hurried behind him, still trying to figure out where the fuck we were.

By the time I got to him, he was already on the porch knocking on the door. I could hear muffled rap music playing inside as we stood there waiting for someone to answer the door. Finally, a beautiful woman came to the door. When she looked out to see who was knocking and saw Kalel, she rolled her eyes and opened the door. It wasn't until she opened the door that I realized that she was the woman that was smoking with me at the club the other night.

"What the fuck you want nigga?" The woman snapped at Kalel.

"Fuck you bitch, I'm here for Deon," Kalel snapped back at her.

She rolled her eyes again and stepped to the side, letting us in the house. When we made eye contact, her demeanor changed quickly. She looked at me as if she almost felt sorry for me, like she knew something I didn't. I just brushed it off.

We finally made it to the basement where the music was coming from. We walked down the stairs and walked into a full-on party. It was niggas and naked women everywhere. I wasn't surprised at all, thinking back to the last outing that I had been on with him previously. I followed behind him like a lost puppy as he slapped fives with a group of guys.

"Damn, this the girl you were telling me about?" One of the guys said as he slapped Kalel five, looking over at me like I was a meal of some sort.

"Yeah, dis her," Kalel replied smiling.

Before I could chime in and ask questions, Kalel grabbed my arm pulling me towards a back room. We came to a small room and the woman that answered the door was there.

"Remi, you got her right?" Kalel asked, now being nice to the woman that he was very rude to prior to that.

"Whatever nigga, come on girl," she replied, rolling her eyes and opening the door letting me into the room.

I hesitantly walked into what looked to be a dressing room, more confused than I was when we pulled up to the house.

"Okay. This spot right here is yours and this is what you are going to be wearing," Remi replied, handing me something that looked like a bunch of string.

"What am I supposed to do with this?" I asked, still confused.

"Change, so you can dance girl. What are you talking about?" Remi replied now picking up on my confusion.

"Dance? What do you mean?"

"He didn't tell you that he was bringing you here to dance for the party?" Remi asked, her face now frowned up.

"No, the fuck he did not!" I snapped, now seeing what was going on.

"Well, I am not in the business of forcing bitches into doing shit that they don't want to, but I know that I am not about to let nobody stop my coins. So, either you get dressed and dance or you can take that up with Kalel," Remi replied with her face frowned up still.

She stormed past me and out of the room. I assumed that it was to get Kalel and get this shit figured out. I stood there looking dumb as fuck trying to figure out what I had gotten myself into the day before my grandmother's funeral. Seconds later, Kalel came in the room alone, closing the door behind him.

"What's up, baby?" Kalel asked, trying to keep his irritation under wraps but doing a very bad job of it.

"What the fuck am I doing here, Kalel?" I snapped, throwing the outfit that Remi had giving me.

"I told you I had a job for you, why you trippin'?" He snapped back at me.

"You didn't fucking tell me that you wanted me to get naked in front of a room full of people I don't know!"

He replied with a smile. "I mean after the other night I thought that was something you were into."

"Kalel, take me the fuck home!" I snapped grabbing my purse standing by the door.

He sat there for a moment, looking at me like he wanted to say something, but he decided against it. Then he stood up and stormed past me, almost hitting me with the door. I followed behind him, just as angry. We passed by the party and out to the truck. We both got in slamming the doors. Kalel started up the truck and pulled off.

"This shit is crazy," I mumbled under my breath.

"As fuck," Kalel replied speeding down the dirt road.

We were silent for the rest of the ride, but you could feel the tension between us. When I saw my apartment, I was overjoyed. Kalel barely parked the truck before my feet were on the ground and I was on my way inside. Just as I walked up to the door, I heard a voice behind me.

"Hey," The voice said.

"Hey." I turned around standing face to face with Anthony.

"You okay?" He asked, stepping closer to the porch and looking over at Kalel's truck that was still sitting in the parking lot.

"I'm fine Anthony, go home," I said looking at the truck.

"I just wanted to make sure that you were good, I can't do that anymore?" He replied looking confused.

"Anthony, please just go home," I begged as I saw Kalel getting out of the truck with something in his hand.

Just as Anthony was turning to look at the truck again, shots rang out. I dropped on the porch screaming and covering my head, praying that I didn't get shot. I heard Anthony yell, then he ran across to his apartment. I watched as he busted through the door. His mother screamed, rushing over to him and looking over at me.

Kalel ran back to the truck and pulled off. I jumped up and ran over to Anthony. Blood ran from his shoulder like water. I grabbed him and pulled him on to my lap as his mother went back and forth with the 911 operator.

"Hey, look at me! You gotta stay with me, Anthony! Please you gotta stay with me!" My tears fell in his face as I rocked back and forth.

He looked up at me, the life slowly starting to leave his eyes as he went in and out of consciousness. His mother finally came back over to us, tears streaming down her face.

"My baby! Come on baby, fight for momma! Please, Anthony, I need you here with me, baby!" She sobbed loudly as the sirens started to get louder in the distance.

"You hear that, Anthony? Help is coming," I said praying to myself that he would be okay.

I was really freaking the fuck out on the inside, hearing the sirens brought back bad memories but I had to keep it together for Anthony.

When the paramedics arrived on the scene, everything felt like it went into fast forward. They snatched Anthony up and put him on a stretcher, working on him immediately taking off to the hospital. His mother got in the ambulance to go with him and I started back to my apartment. I could hear the police sirens getting closer. I got in the house as fast as I could, snatching my stuff up from the porch.

I watched from the window as the lights slowed up in front of my house, then slowly pulled away. I exhaled loudly as I headed to the bathroom to take a shower and wash off all the blood that was on me. I cried as I waited for the water to get hot. I couldn't believe that Kalel was crazy enough to shoot at Anthony for talking to me. Knowing that I was going to have to cut Anthony out of my life for real now was the part that hurt the most. I never wanted anything to happen to him or his mom and I knew that as long as I was keeping in contact with Anthony, I put both of them in danger.

I got in the shower, scrubbing Anthony's blood off of me watching it run down the drain. That only made me cry harder. After about 45 minutes of hardcore bawling, I finished my shower and stepped out grabbing the towel from the rack and wrapping it around me. I walked back into the living room and sat on the couch. I grabbed my purse that I had thrown on the table when I came in. I pulled out my bag of weed and my bag of cocaine, sitting it on the table before going back in my purse to find a blunt wrap. I finally found one hidden under my phone. I flung the purse on the couch and rolled up a fat ass blunt. I was in such a hurry to get high and leave all the bullshit behind that I lit the blunt before it could even dry.

I took two long drags off of it and sat it in the ashtray, laying back on the couch and letting the drugs take effect. As tears began running down my face again, I sighed loudly thinking about how my life was falling apart. Now Anthony was in the hospital because of me and I had to get up and lay my grandmother to rest the next morning with all that on my mind.

I knew that I wouldn't hear from Kalel until shit blew over, so I was alone. I looked at the little drug stash that I had left, trying to measure if I could stretch it or not. I grabbed my blunt and hit it again. That hit put me on my ass for real. I dropped it back in the ashtray and laid back as my eyes rolled and closed. My body finally relaxed, and I drifted off to sleep.

The next morning, my alarm woke me up. I set it once the arrangements were set for my grandmother's service. I got up, scratching my head. The car was going to be pulling up in an hour, so I got up, realizing that I was still in my towel. I walked in my room grabbing the black dress that was hanging on my bedroom door, tossing it on my bed. I reached into my top drawer and grabbed my pantyhose and a clean pair of panties. Just as I was sliding the dress down over my body, there was a knock at the door.

I walked towards the door taking a deep breath in

case it was Kalel coming back to finish the job. When I opened the door, Setra was standing on my porch crying.

"Oh my God Setra, is Anthony okay?" I asked panicking.

"Yes, the doctor just called, he said that they finally got him stable," She replied, smiling wide.

"That is great," I replied hugging her.

"I was just coming to check on you. I know that today is a hard day," She replied rubbing my hand.

"I mean, this is never something that I thought I would be doing so soon, but I can't control any of this," I replied hanging my head.

"Well, you look, beautiful sweetheart."

"Thank you so much," I replied half smiling.

"Okay, I will see you at the church," She said, turning and walking off the porch back towards her apartment.

I closed the door, thanking God that Setra didn't ask me what happened. I couldn't look her in the face and tell her that I was the reason her son got shot. I headed back to my bedroom to finish getting ready for the service. Another knock at the door snatched my attention. I walked back to the door, snatching it open.

"I'm sure you don't have anything to say to me, but it wouldn't have been right for me to let you go through this day alone," Bear said, looking up at me from the bottom step of the porch.

"Come in Bear." I walked away from the door, leaving it open.

He walked into the apartment, closing the door behind him and sitting on the couch. I grabbed my shoes out of my bedroom and sat next to him on the couch.

"I'm sorry," I blurted out stepping into my shoes.

"No need to apologize. I know things have been really rough lately," He replied looking over at me.

"Yeah, all this bullshit is clouding my judgment."

"Your mouth," He replied laughing.

"What?" I asked laughing as well.

"There is never a dull moment with you," Bear replied.

"Well come on. Let's enjoy this little sunlight until the family car gets here," I said heading towards the door.

Bear followed me to the porch and sat down on the step.

"Look, I know that I can't take you in and everything, but you know that I will always look out for you." Bear patted my leg.

"I know Bear," I replied smiling.

I was happy that we were back on good terms because I needed someone to help me through all the shit that had dropped at my feet. I sat there thinking about the blunt that I had in the ashtray, knowing that I wouldn't be able to curb my hunger for the drug until I was alone since no one, but Kalel knew about my habit.

I noticed the family car pulling up in the parking lot. I tapped Bear on the arm, letting him know the car was there as I got up and went back in the apartment to get my purse and my drugs. I snatched the blunt out of the ashtray, sticking it in the bag with the rest of the weed that I had and stuffed both in my purse and left out of the apartment.

We climbed into the car and headed to the church. I stared out of the window watching the Detroit streets go by, looking at the hood that raised me, remembering all the shit that I had done in the streets and how the people that were around then were nowhere to be found now.

# ANTHONY

Things had been rough since Ms. Mary passed away, then my mother had to go to the funeral without me by her side. My mother's drinking had picked up drastically since everything had taken place. I knew shit was bad when I came home from the hospital and the house was completely trashed. My mother had always been a clean woman, so I knew things were getting worse.

I tried my best to be as helpful as I could with my bad shoulder. I cooked and cleaned whatever she needed to try and keep things afloat while we worked on getting her better. I saw Alex once while I was in the hospital, but it was just for her to tell me that she couldn't talk to me anymore to keep me and my mother safe.

Honestly, I wasn't afraid of Kalel. To me, he was just another low-balling ass neighborhood dope boy that was nickel and dimein' his life away. I worried about Alex being with him because I didn't want anything to happen to her being with him, but I couldn't make her do what I wanted her to do. I couldn't focus on her life and take care of my mother and my injury thinking about her every moment of the day, so when I saw her at the hospital, I knew that I had to close that chapter for now. I told myself that if it was meant to be, then it would be.

I started to miss a lot of school due to my living situation. My mother was so drunk all the time that she didn't even notice. It was almost like she was used to me being there and taking care of her. One morning I was cooking her breakfast and she came into the kitchen with a weird look on her face.

"Good morning baby boy," she said, pulling a chair

from the dining room to the kitchen.

"Good morning Ma. Why the serious face?" I asked, checking on the eggs that I was making for her.

"I just have a lot on my mind, baby."

"I have nothing but time," I shot back at her.

"I'm just going through a lot, missing your father and then with Ms. Mary passing away the way she did. I just keep thinking about the fact that I wasn't there with her and she had to go through that by herself," she replied, wiping the tears that had started to run down her face.

"Ma, you can't beat yourself up about that. I'm sure that Ms. Mary never looked at it that way she loved you and you loved her. That's what matters most." I was doing my best to keep her spirits up.

I hated seeing my mother like that, so down and defeated. She honestly felt like she had failed Ms. Mary. At first it pissed me off because I always felt like the person that should be feeling that way was sleeping like a baby every night.

"I should have been there," my mother sobbed, shaking her head.

I finished cooking her breakfast and sat everything on the table for her to eat. She pulled the chair that she had been sitting in, to the table. I sat in the chair next to her to finish our conversation.

"Ma stop beating yourself up. It wasn't your fault or anyone's fault for that matter."

"Let's just drop it okay. What are your plans for the day?" She attempted to eat her breakfast.

"Well, I really didn't have any. I still have a little pain when I use my shoulder too much, so I was just gon' chill with you today," I replied going back into the kitchen to pour her a glass of orange juice.

"Nah baby. Get out and get you some sunlight." Ma smiled at me and patting my cheek.

"You sure, Ma?" I asked confused.

"Yes, go live your life baby boy." She got up and went into her bedroom, closing the door behind her.

I sat on the couch for a minute before I decided to go out and sit on the porch. As I was coming out of the house, Bianca was walking past. She looked at me and kept walking then she stopped and came back.

"You look like shit." Her voice reeked of sarcasm.

"You would know," I replied, looking up at her.

She started laughing and walked over, sitting on the porch.

"How are you?" Bianca pointed to my shoulder.

"I'm taking it a day at a time, thanks for asking. What's got you talking to me?" I ask blatantly.

"I just told myself I needed to let that shit go. I mean you might have said some mean shit to me once or twice, but I am a big girl. I can handle it. I mean either way you ain't switched up," she replied.

"That's real. So what's been up? You talk to Alex?" I asked.

She shook her head. "Nah, I really don't have too much to say to her. I tried talking to her, but Alex is another person since she got with Kalel."

"Yeah, I feel like that, too. Hopefully, she pulls her shit together before it's too late," I replied hating that there was nothing I could do to help her.

"Anthony, can I ask you a question?" Bianca asked.

"Shoot," I replied propping my feet on the porch railing.

"What was it about me that made you not want to talk to me?" She asked with a straight face.

"Honestly, it was the man-bashing. Like if a guy didn't make a certain amount of money he was a bum and you made it very clear that bum niggas were not ya thing," I replied laughing.

She hung her head. "I did say that, but that was a front I didn't want to be looked at as the bitch in the projects that had the broke nigga that couldn't do nothing for her."

"Why does what another says matter so much to you?" I asked confused.

"When you come from where I come from, your reputation is how you survive," she replied wiping the sweat that started to bead up in her forehead.

"I guess I can see that. What made you ask?" I asked.

She smirked. "Because I like you. I have always liked you and I just feel like if you gave me a chance to show you who I really am, that you could grow to love me."

In the beginning, I really did look at Bianca as one of the neighborhood rats and I had always felt like she was in competition with Alex when it came to me. Since she and Alex had not been talking, I had been seeing a different side of her even if it was in passing. I figured I couldn't sit around and wait my whole life on Alex.

"Well, what do you have to do right now? We could run over to Pizza Papoulis and get something to eat if you want," I said nervously, waiting to hear her answer.

"I'm cool with that. Let me go get my purse and I will be right back," She jumped up off of the porch and skipped to her house.

I sat there waiting for her to get back as I battled with myself about my actions. Was I wrong for wondering if I had Bianca pegged all wrong from the beginning and wanting to see who she really was? I mean, I had been so stuck on Alex that I had really never given Bianca a second look. It didn't have to be a date or a relationship, I just really needed to get away from everything that was going on in my life at the moment. Bianca's silhouette pulled me from my thoughts. I threw a fake smile on to keep her from asking questions.

"Look, if this is going to be hard for you or have you feeling some type of way, then we don't have to go." Bianca saw right through my façade.

"It's nothing like that. Let me just go get my mom's keys. I'll be right back." I kicked myself in the ass for not hiding my feelings better as I walked into the house.

"Aye Ma, is it cool if I take the truck to grab something to eat?" I called out to her.

"The keys are in the bowl on the table," she said through her bedroom door.

I had gotten my L's just before I got shot. That's what I was trying to tell Alex the night of the shooting. That was perfect for my mother because I was able to start running her errands which kept her in the house, just like she liked it. I grabbed the keys out of the bowl and headed back out to Bianca.

"Ready?" I asked locking up the house behind me.

Bianca smiled widely. "Ready."

We walked to the truck. I opened her door for her,

closing it once she was in. I walked around and jumped in the driver seat.

"So, tell me something about you that I don't know," Bianca said breaking the silence in the truck.

"I think you know it all really. What about you?"

I wasn't all that interesting if I had to say so myself, so whatever she was looking for, she wasn't going to get it today.

"Well, I always wanted to have a big wedding and a bunch of kids," she replied looking out of the window.

"I would have never thought that."

"I get that all the time."

I pulled into the restaurant parking lot and parked right by the door. I got out, opened Bianca's door and then we headed into the restaurant. The host greeted us and walked us to our table. We climbed into the booth and continued our conversation.

"There is one thing that I do want to know," I blurted out as we got comfortable.

"What's that?" She asked.

"When did your feelings for me get this strong?" I was curious to hear her answer.

"Really, the day you moved in. I was sitting on the porch with Kila the girl that used to live three doors down from you the day you moved in. You looked like you kept to yourself, not like all the other dudes in the projects always looking for the next money bag they can rob," she replied candidly.

I grinned. "That's a respectable answer, I guess."

"You are not like anyone that I have ever had in my life." Bianca was now staring me in my eyes.

I was almost sucked in until I thought about the fact that Bianca had a crush on Kalel before Alex got with him. She could have been using me to get back at Alex.

"Why are you doing this?" I asked with a straight face.

"What do you mean?"

"Is this your way of getting back at Alex for getting with Kalel?" I was ready to get up and leave.

"Anthony it's not like that. I swear, I really do like you. I always have and you know that," Bianca replied, offended.

I wasn't trying to be a dick, I just saw how shit was falling together and I knew that if I found out that she was playing me, shit wasn't going to be pretty.

"Nah, my bad. I shouldn't have come at you like that."

"I mean I can't blame you for thinking like that, but, as I told you before, I put all that behind me."

I figured I had nothing to lose trying things out with Bianca. I never knew how things would end up and looking at the way that stuff had recently been going, it was time for me to put everything that I thought was for me, behind me.

# ALEX

Three days after I laid my grandmother to rest there was a knock at the door. I got out of the bed dragging my feet as I made my way to the door, pulling it open slowly.

"Good morning Alex, may I come in?" Samantha said with a phony smile.

I stepped back, opening the door and letting her into the apartment.

"Came to take me away?" I asked sarcastically.

"I came to inform you that tomorrow morning you will be moving into the local girls' home in your area, so anything that you want to take, you need to pack tonight," Samantha said with an attitude.

"Why not today?" I asked prying for information.

She scrunched her eyebrows. "They have to get a bed ready for you and that takes at least a day.".

"Okay. I will make sure that I have everything ready," I replied smiling, walking Samantha back towards the door.

"I will be here at 9 am, so be up, ready and looking presentable," She said as she walked out of the apartment.

As soon as she cleared the threshold I slammed the

door. I ran to my bedroom, grabbed my duffle bag from under the bed and packed anything that I thought I would need, starting with my clothes. I grabbed my phone and called Kalel. I hadn't talked to him since the shooting, but I had to get the fuck on and fast. He picked up on the first ring.

"I thought you ain't fuck with me no more," he grumbled into the phone.

"Feeling guilty?" I asked sarcastically, still packing.

"A little. Wanna go eat and talk about it?" He asked, sounding hopeful.

"You know what, that would actually be a great idea." I quickly thought about how he was doing my job for me. I really wasn't trying to fuck with him anymore, but I needed him.

"A'ight, I'm on my way," Kalel said.

"Okay daddy," I replied, ending the call and shoving my phone in my pocket and getting back to my packing.

I grabbed all my bags and headed to the door. I stopped just before I walked out of the apartment, looking at what had been my home for 3 years. I felt the tears building up in my eyes. I wiped them quickly and walked out of the apartment, dropping my bag on the porch as I closed the door. Kalel pulled up before I could even sit on the step. He got out of the truck and came over to help me get my bags off of the porch.

I jumped in the truck and closed my door as Kalel put the rest of my bags in the trunk. I took one last look at my home as Kalel put the truck in gear and pulled out of the parking lot. I took some deep breaths to keep the tears that wanted to pour out of me at bay.

"You okay?" He quizzed, looking over at me with a concerned stare on his face.

"Yeah, I'm cool I guess, but to be honest, I really don't want to go out to eat. I just wanna chill and get fucked up," I replied with a sigh.

"I know shit seems like it's fucked up bad right now, but you know I got you right?" He grabbed my hand.

"I guess you're right," I replied, smiling at him.

"You know what, I got just the thing for you, and we can just go to the crib and order some takeout." He reached into the middle console and pulled out half a blunt, handing it to me with a lighter.

I took the blunt and lit it. Taking a long drag off of it cracking my window, instantly I could tell that he had come across the same drug mix that I was already into. We rode deeper into the city headed to his apartment. By the time we got there I was high out of my mind and ready to give Kalel something he could feel for real. He parked the truck and threw me the keys so I could open the door while he got my bags.

I walked into the apartment and grabbed the lighter that was sitting on the arm of the couch and re-lit the blunt that had gone out in the car. I hit it again, letting the drug take control of the mood. Kalel came in shortly after with all my shit. He took my bags into the bedroom and then came back in the living room, flopping down on the couch. I flopped next to him passing him the blunt.

"So, what's going on with you?" He asked hitting the blunt.

"Before my grandmother's funeral, Samantha came to the door talking that foster care shit and I wasn't trying to hear that. She came back just before we talked earlier telling me that tomorrow morning I was going to the girls' home and I wasn't trying to hear that shit. So, I ran and that's how I ended up here," I replied taking the blunt from his hand as he passed it back to me.

"That shit is crazy as fuck. You are grown, why can't you just stay in the apartment and get your paperwork to be your own guardian?" He asked.

I was shocked that he knew how shit worked for real. I never took him for a book reader, but it was nice to know that he really did have a brain.

"She said it was because I wasn't 17 yet," I replied, rolling my eyes and passing the blunt back to him.

He laid his head back on the couch and put his hand on my thigh.

"Well, you here with me now and I am going to make sure that we're straight." Kalel moved his hand up my thigh, sending a chill up my spine.

"What are you doing?" I asked with a giggle.

A mischievous grin graced his lips. "Shid, whatever you let me."

I could see that living with Kalel was going to be fun and I was looking forward to making my money and living my life the way I wanted to. I just wish that I could call Anthony from time to time. I was starting to miss his company and I really hoped that he was okay after the shooting.

"Earth to Alex, you still with me?" Kalel asked, snatching me out of my thoughts.

"My bad I was in my head." I laughed nervously as he reached over and rubbed my face.

"Why don't you come in the room and let me take your mind off of whatever got yo attention like this." I watched as Kalel got up and headed to the bedroom.

Kalel was seven years older than me, so he was a lot more experienced then I was in the bedroom, so I was just going to let him lead the way. I hadn't been out in the world long but from the conversations that I had heard, pussy was the way to any man's heart. I needed him and I knew he would want something in return, so it was time for me to pay up in the pussy department.

I grinned as I got up and followed him. Before he could get around the corner, he was out of his shirt. I followed his lead, peeling my shirt off as well. He turned and grabbed me by my waist, lifting me off my feet. I took this as an opening and wrapped my legs around him. He kissed me passionately holding me tighter, I started to feel something for Kalel that I had never felt before.

It was like he was handling me differently than he usually would. He was gentler and took his time getting me in the mood. He kissed my neck softly as he caressed my back and ass, putting me up against the bedroom wall. I threw my head back on the wall and let out a low moan.

"I love the way you moan," Kalel whispered seductively.

"I love the way you make me moan daddy," I replied licking my lips and kissing him again.

He walked me over to the bed letting me down gently. I undid the button on my pants and slid them down over my feet as if I was putting on a peep show for him, dropping them on the side of the bed. Kalel stood there smiling as I continued to put on my show. He caressed my legs and thighs, kissing my feet and ankles.

"Why are you still in clothes?" I asked biting my bottom lip.

Kalel smiled harder as he began to undo his belt and drop his pants and boxers to his ankles, revealing his anaconda that was big as fuck already and it wasn't even all the way hard. I sized him up feeling my heartbeat starting to pick up. Kalel wasn't all that cute in the face, but between his body that was beautifully put together and his big ass dick, he was great in my book.

I watched his muscles flex as he leaned down to kiss my stomach and chest before dropping to his knees and parting mine slowly. I laid my head back and braced myself for what was about to happen. As soon as his lips touch my pussy, my body melted, and I came all over the place. Kalel busted out laughing and grabbed my legs, pulling me closer to the end of the bed so that he could comfortably finish his meal.

He slid his tongue across my clit, flicking my little button causing me to cry out.

"You like that shit don't you?" He shoved his face deeper into my box.

"Mm, yes baby, don't stop," I replied, running my fingers through his little baby fro.

He munched on my box like he hadn't eaten in years, pinning my legs down so I couldn't run. I was losing my mind trying to hold back and keep my stamina. I could feel my juices starting to run down my ass.

"Fuck, I'm cummin!" I cried out.

"Dat's right, come, fah daddy," Kalel replied, sliding two of his fingers inside of me.

"Mm, Kalel," I cried out as I exploded all over him for a second time.

"You ready for this dick?" He was now standing over me stroking his dick. I was too busy trying to catch my breath.

"I'm always ready for you baby," I replied smiling.

He put my feet up on his shoulders as he lined up ready to beat down my guts. I took a deep breath as the anticipation was starting to get the best of me. He pushed the tip in and that was all she wrote. Immediately, he went to banging my shit to a pulp so much so, that by the third pump, I was hollering. I could hear our bodies slapping together as we continued our hardcore fuck session.

"Damn, this shit tight as fuck girl!" Kalel cried out as I started to feel his muscle jump, letting me know that he was close to his blowing point.

I tightened my pussy muscles and tilted my hips back. Kalel went crazy digging his nails into my thigh, making me wince a little.

"I'm about to bust!" Kalel cried out, pulling out and spilling his babies all over my stomach.

I giggled as the warm liquid ran down my stomach and my sides.

"You goin fuck around and make a nigga wife you girl," he said, sitting on the side of the bed, lighting another blunt and hitting it.

"I thought that was the plan?" I asked pulling the sheet over me and snuggling up behind him.

"I guess we will have to see how this shit go huh?".

"What the fuck is that supposed to mean?" I asked offended.

"Exactly what the fuck I just said," Kalel snapped back at me.

"What type of bitch do you take me for?" I spat at him, getting up from the bed and wrapping up in the sheet.

"The bitch that is going to do what the fuck I tell you to do!" He shouted, jumping up from the bed as well.

"Or what?" I asked sarcastically.

Before I could understand what was happening, Kalel jumped across the bed and slapped the shit out of me. I fell to the floor seeing stars. I couldn't believe that he had just hit me like that. I was afraid that he would hit me again, so I laid there holding my face. I could hear him moving around the room and then the next thing I heard was the front door open and slam shut.

I sat up, tears streaming down my face. I would have never in a million years thought that he would do something like that to me. I had never heard of him putting his hands on any of the other chicks that he had been with. All I knew was that if his plan was to scare the shit out of me it worked for sure. I got back in the bed and balled up, I wanted to leave but I had nothing and no one so I was stuck. I laid there crying my eyes out until my eyelids got too heavy to continue to hold them open.

***

The next morning, I jumped out of my sleep dreaming about the events of the night before. I was still in the bed the way that I had been when I laid down. My face was dry and crusty, and Kalel still hadn't come back. I sat up and looked at the clock on his dresser; it was 8 am. I got up, holding the sheet to keep it wrapped around me and went to the living room to get my phone out of my jacket. I dialed his number. It rang once and went to voicemail. Just as I was turning to go back in the bedroom, I heard him coming in the door.

I stop in my tracks and turned around, waiting for him to come in. When the door opened and Kalel walked in, I hesitated before I said anything.

"Where were you?" I asked nervously.

"Look I'm sorry about last night, but don't question me," he said, brushing past me and going into the bathroom, turning on the shower. I stood there for a moment watching as he walked back and forth gathering the things he needed to take a shower. I was in awe. I almost let my mouth fall open, but I caught myself. It was like he had turned into another person overnight and I didn't like where shit was going.

"I can just go," I finally got out, catching him in passing.

He looked at me like I had just told him that his mother ate monkey balls all her life. He started walking towards me and I started backing up. Kalel backed me up against the door and leaned down in my ear.

"You ain't going nowhere. Don't nobody want you, that's why you here, right? Try it, just go ahead and try it and I will make your life a living hell," he whispered in my ear, walking back into the bathroom.

It instantly got to my stomach. I went from living my best life, to becoming a prisoner and I wasn't going to call his bluff because I really didn't think that he was bluffing. Aside from the fact that even though his words were harsh, they held a lot of truth. I was there because I didn't have anyone to take me in, so I had to keep my shit together if I wanted a safe place to sleep every night. I went back into the bedroom and grabbed my bag to look for something to put on. I grabbed my long nightgown and pulled it over my head. I went back into the kitchen to find something to eat as I waited for Kalel to come out of the bathroom.

By the time he actually surfaced, I was finished eating my bowl of cereal that I had conjured up. He walked into the living room and sat down on the couch. I put my bowl in the sink and went to sit with him.

"Did you pay for the food that you just ate?" He asked, hitting the blunt in his hand.

"Pay for it? What do you mean?" I asked, confused.

"Ain't shit in this life free, not even food. You owe me." He never even looked me in the face.

"So, how do you expect me to do that, Kalel? You know I don't have any money," I rolled my eyes at him.

"Be ready tonight at 8p.m. Once you pay me for that meal, you can keep everything else that you make." He got up and went into the bedroom, closing the door behind him as a gesture that he didn't want me to follow him.

I laid back on the couch and grabbed the remote, remembering that I still had a little stash of my own since I could see that Kalel wasn't in a sharing mood. I grabbed my purse out of the chair and pulled out my weed and cocaine mixture, hoping that there was also a wrap in there as well. I guess the drug gods heard my plea because all the way at the bottom of my purse, I found one.

I rolled the blunt as fast as I could, lighting it immediately, trying to get away from all the emotions that I was going through. As soon as the drugs hit my system, I was free. I could feel all my problems lifting off of me the higher I got. Once the blunt was gone, I laid on the couch with tears running down my face as I broke down internally. I laid there, staring at the ceiling and letting the drugs take me wherever they deemed for me to go.

***

At about 7 p.m., Kalel emerged from the bedroom half-dressed. I was still laying in the same spot from earlier staring at the ceiling, so when he came out I already knew what it was about.

"Time to get up and get dressed pretty girl," he tapped my foot, thinking I was asleep like nothing had ever happened.

"What am I supposed to wear?" I asked dryly, not really feeling him.

"Your clothes are on the bed," Kalel walked into the bathroom.

I got up and went into the bedroom to find a cute little sexy black two-piece outfit, paired with a pair of black leather thigh-high boots that tied in the back. I was still admiring the clothes that Kalel had picked out for me when he came back into the bedroom, wrapping his arms around my waist kissing me on the neck.

"What do you think?" He asked, kissing me on the ear this time.

"I like it, but where are my underwear?" I pulled away from him and grabbed my bag to find some.

Kalel could tell that I wasn't really feeling him at the moment. I was still reeling from him putting his hands on me. I mean, I could deal with what seemed like really bad mood swings, but I couldn't deal with being beaten up by someone I called my boyfriend.

"Look, I owe you an apology for last night. I should have never put my hands on you like that, and I promise it won't happen again," he said while rubbing my cheek.

I smiled up at him. "I am going to hold you to that."

"I am going to let you."

I don't really know if it was the fact that he was man enough to see that he was wrong and apologize, or the fact that he cared enough to apologize, but that moment changed my whole mood. I went from being mad and afraid, back to my regular self in a flash. I jumped up, kissed Kalel on the lips and bounced into the bathroom to clean myself up.

By 8 p.m. on the dot, I was walking out of the

bedroom fully dressed. Kalel looked up at me when I walked into the living room, sitting next to him to tie my boots.

"Damn Alex, you looking good girl," He said smiling wide.

"Thank you, you were dead on with my sizes," I replied blushing and twirling around so he could see the whole outfit.

"That just lets you know I pay attention," He passed me the blunt that he had lit.

I took it from him, taking a few long drags before giving it back.

"So now that I'm dressed, I just have to worry about my hair," I said thinking out loud.

"No, you don't. I have all the rest taken care of already. We just need to get out of here." He got up and grabbed his shoes, sliding his feet into them before grabbing his keys.

I grabbed my jacket and my purse and followed him out the door. We jumped in the truck and we were on our way.

"Here, light this. You going to want to be high tonight," he said, handing me the blunt that had gone out in the transition from the apartment to the truck.

I did as he said and sat back in my seat as I smoked

myself into oblivion. When I started to notice that the streets that we were riding on looked familiar, I snapped back to reality, but with my new-found knowledge of who Kalel could be, I decided it was best for me to just keep my mouth closed.

When we turned down the dirt road, I knew for sure that we were going back to the house he had taken me to some time before. When we pulled up to the house he threw the truck in park and got out. I put the blunt in the ashtray and got out as well. I threw my jacket and my purse back in the truck and closed the door, jogging slightly to catch up to him. Remi was standing at the door smoking a black n mild when we walked up on the porch.

"What yo' broke ass want," she shot at Kalel the moment she saw him.

"Here you go with yo shit. Shut yo bald head ass up talking to me," He replied brushing past her and walking in the house with me on his tail.

We went straight to the basement as we did before, only this time the party wasn't as big as the last time we had been here. Once again Kalel walked through slapping fives a dapping niggas' up. By then Remi had come back to the party, Kalel motioned for me to go with her but before I walked away he pulled me back and whispered in my ear.

"We not goin do the same shit as last time unless you

want me to break your fucking face. Now go make us some money," he replied damn near pushing me into Remi as she led me back to what I now knew for sure was a dressing room.

I tried to play it off like I felt no type of way, but Remi could see it all over my face. She wasted no time speaking on it when we got in the dressing room out of earshot of everyone else.

"So how long he been beating yo ass?" She asked candidly.

"What are you talking about? He has never put his hands on me," I lied, hoping that she would leave well enough alone.

"Listen, you are a beautiful girl and I don't know how you ended up with a scumbag like Kalel, but if I was you, the moment I made enough money to get the fuck on, I would. That nigga is no good to anybody and he definitely goin work you over as long as you keep playing yo self," she said, tossing me another skanky outfit to put on.

I took the outfit off the hanger and held it in my hand for a moment, wishing I was somewhere else. Remi walked over to me and put her hand on my shoulder.

"Here, drink this. It should take the edge off." Remi handed me a glass with a dark brown substance in it.

I took the glass and dumped the contents in my mouth and swallowed fast, exhaling as my chest started to burn.

"What the fuck was that?" I said wiping my mouth trying to make the horrible taste go away.

"Hennessy. You mean to tell me you ain't never had it before?" Remi held a shocked look on her face.

"Nah, drinking was never really my thing. I mean none of this shit was my thing until my grandmother died," I replied, letting my own words settle as I came out of my clothes to put on the outfit.

Usually, I would have wanted to be alone to get dressed, but with the little strings and dangles that were on the outfit, I was going to need some help.

"Damn I am so sorry to hear that, but now is not the time for your life story. You got money to make right now girl. When I have a party that I really don't want to do, I find a way to make it easy. I picture all them niggas as dollar bills, naked fucking dollar bills," Remi replied proudly laughing at herself.

I let out a small laugh, still trying to shake the butterflies that were going nuts in my stomach.

"Here take another shot," she replied as she helped me into the outfit.

I took the glass from her and dumped the contents in my mouth as I had done before. This time around my toes started to tingle and my body started to feel more relaxed. Even though I wasn't a drinking Remi's remedies worked just fine.

"Damn, that shit really works," I said giggling goofily.

"I told you," She replied laughing.

Before any more time could be wasted, someone knocked on the door. Remi snatched it open to find Kalel and another guy on the other side of the door. When Kalel caught a glimpse of me in my new outfit, his face lit up. He smiled wider than I had ever seen before. Even though I didn't really want to be doing what I was doing, seeing him happy like that did something to me and it almost made everything okay.

"What's up, what's taking so long?" The other guy asked Remi.

"Don't come in here rushing nothing Deon, I got this," Remi snapped at him.

"Look, don't show out in front of company," He spat back at her.

"Yeah nigga, whateva." She closed the door in their faces and returned back to me and our original task.

"Them niggas killing me. All they care about is pussy and money," I said in a low tone.

"Well if we were wired like they are we would be the same way, but on some real shit, this party is starting to pick up. Get out there and get yo money boo, you got this," Remi said smiling at me.

I took a deep breath and looked at the door before I walked over and opened it and stepped back into the party. Remi caught me before I could get all the way out of the dressing room.

"Hey, what you want me to call you and what you wanna dance to?" She asked.

I had never even thought about any of that, so I stood there for a moment before I answered.

"Just call me by my name, Alex, and play something ratchet for me," I replied, pulling my confidence together and walking out of the room.

Remi's voice came over the mic to introduce me and let everyone know that the show was about to start.

*"What's good wit you wack ass niggas tonight! This ya girl Remi Rem on the ones and twos and I am running this bitch tonight. So Y'all all know that when I host some shit, its goin be lit as fuck. So, pull out ya stacks and make it rain for my girl Alex. She bout to make that shit clap and bring this bitch down!"*

With that, *No Panties* by Mulatto came blasting through the speakers and everyone started to crowd around me. I started shaking my ass as I dropped on my knees making it clap fast. I could tell that the two shots that Remi had given me were starting to course through me for real as I started to let go of all my fear that I had initially. I crawled across the basement floor, making sure to poke my ass out so it could be seen.

Kalel was the first one to pull a wad of money out of his pocket and throw some ones at me as I wiggled and gyrated all over the floor. I rolled my body up slowly trying to be as sexy as I could. I needed all the money I could get. I was so focused on not fucking shit up that I had tuned out all the shouting that was going on around me as they lost their minds over my body. It wasn't until I started to feel the bills raining down on my skin that I snapped back to reality, realizing that I was laying in a pool of money.

Before I knew it the song was over, and my job was done. Remi helped me put all the money in a big garbage bag and take it back to the dressing room. When we got in the dressing room, I lost it. I was so excited and amped up.

"That's what the fuck I'm talking about, bitch! Take these niggas money! They don't need it, shit, they don't even know what to do with it." She slapped me five and handed me another shot.

"Period bitch," I replied smiling wide, taking the shot

and shooting it right away. This time the burn didn't even bother me like before.

"You smoke?" She asked passing me the blunt.

"Hell yeah," I replied taking the blunt from her dragging it hard as I could. It was well needed.

"I like you. Here, put my number in your phone. I'm about to call you so you can have mine," Remi pulled her phone out of her pocket.

I gave her my phone number and locked her in.

"I can't believe that I made all this money off one song," I said too geeked.

"Wait till you do the next one," She replied.

"The next one?" I asked as my eyebrow went up.

"Yeah, at parties like this I try to do two songs because by then these niggas are just drunk enough to give you everything they got. By the third one, they too drunk to think and you can go home with all the money you made earlier in the night," Remi replied.

"Well, since you put it that way, when's the next one?" I asked, geared up for the next dance.

"Come on, you know I got you," She replied opening the dressing door walking out with me following behind.

Remi climbed back into the DJ section and grabbed the mic again.

*"Alright muthafuckas, that was cute how ya'll just*

*made it rain off in this bitch, but I need all the niggas on the floor with some real money. She ain't no cheap bitch you wanna see ass shaking and pussy twerking its goin cost some cheese so bring that shit the fuck out for my girl Alex! Aye DJ drop that shit nigga!"*

And just like that, another beat dropped, and I was back at it. I was sucked in and it was no going back. Once again, everyone crowded around me as I worked for my money. The second time felt like it went fast then the first time, but I was cool with that because I had one job when I walked into the party, I came to make my money and like that it was over.

By the end of the night, I was leaving the party with three garbage bags full of money and Kalel was happy as hell. As long as we were happy, that was all I cared about. I said my goodbyes to Remi once Kalel had put all the money in the truck and we were on our way home before I knew it.

"Damn girl, that shit was crazy, and you looked sexy as hell," Kalel gushed as we rode down the dirt road.

"Thanks, baby," I replied blushing.

"So, when you wanna do it again?" He glanced over at me.

"Whenever I can," I smiled, thinking about what I had just done and all the money that I made.

"Shit. I can make it so you doing it every night if you want," Kalel's grin widened.

"After this shit, I'm game for all that shit."

Kalel had no idea that I was sucked in and he had created a monster. The money came so fast and easy that in my mind, it wasn't any other way for me to get this kind of money faster, so this was it. I didn't have any other plans and I was great at this shit. Fuck school and all that other shit that people always tried to force me to believe would make me a living. Stripping was my living now, and that was it.

# ANTHONY

My mother drank herself into the hospital with a dying liver and many other health issues that we had no idea would pan out, leaving me to tend to everything until she came home. Bianca had been by my side every step of the way. Things between us had gotten real and I loved it all., She was nothing like the person that I had made her out to be in my head. I dropped out of school and got a part-time job hoping to keep a roof over my head. Bianca would go to the apartment after she got out of school, cook and clean the apartment.

She was such a beautiful person on the inside, that I would often kick myself in the ass for almost missing out on a good girl. She would go sit at the hospital with my mother while I was at work and on days where I was dog ass tired from working and couldn't find the energy to go myself. She would stay the night with me at the apartment a couple of nights out of the week just so I wouldn't be alone in my thoughts, which I thought was dope as fuck because she had no idea how many nights I didn't sleep. All and all, she was a dope ass girlfriend and I was glad that we decided to give this shit a try.

123

I hadn't heard from Alex since I saw her at the hospital. I knew it would be like this once she told me that she couldn't talk to me anymore to keep me and my mother safe. I couldn't lie and say that because I was with Bianca that I didn't think about Alex, or even that I didn't miss her from time to time. Every time I would think about her though, I would hear my grandmother in my head telling me that what was for me was going to be for me and there was nothing that could stop that. So, when Alex popped into my head, I would try to get her out as fast as possible or I go do something with Bianca and give her that energy. I mean shit, she deserved it. Alex was off living her best life and she probably wasn't even thinking about me.

Valentine's Day was getting ready to roll around and I had to come up with something to do for Bianca. My mother was always getting free hotel rooms at the casino since she and her friends went all the time before her drinking got too bad for her to drive. I decided to book one and surprise Bianca. Of course, I had to use someone that was over 18 to get it for me, but it all worked out. I had been putting money away from my paychecks for a rainy-day fund, so I had the money for the deposit. Then, the only thing I had to do was get her hair and nails done and get all the stuff that we needed for the night without her knowing.

Three days before Valentine's Day, my cousin Rock

came into town. I was still sleeping when he showed up pounding on the apartment door. I was pissed that I was snatched from my sleep, so when I snatched the door open I had no intention of being nice until I saw it was him.

"My nigga Ant!" He shouted loudly, reaching out to slap me five.

"Aw shit what up Rock!"

Rock was always the cousin that had my back no matter what. He was three years older than me so when niggas would fuck with me he would be there to fuck them up. Of course, as we got older our lives went in different directions but that never changed the bond that we had built. My mother would always complain about us hanging out because she didn't want me caught up in the street life and that was all Rock knew.

"What the fuck is up, nigga! You goin' let me in, or you got some little breezy in there?" He asked, trying to see into the apartment.

"Nah, I sent my girl home last night to try and finish up these Valentine's Day plans," I told him, stepping to the side to let him in.

"Oh, okay my nigga. I see you a ladies' man out here. What are you trying to do for her?" He sat on the couch and pulled out his blunt.

"Shit, I was trying to get one of the rooms at Motor City, but you know that shit probably booked up and I'm not 18 yet, so I gotta find somebody to book it for me," I replied looking dumb.

"Aww nigga don't you worry about that. I can set up some shit fah you nigga."

"Dat would be clutch as fuck my nigga," I replied slapping him five.

"Listen, when you got a good one, you gotta treat her like a queen. You headed in the right direction. Oh yeah, I saw ya girl Alex a little while ago at one of Remi's parties.".

"Oh yeah? She always been the turn-up type. How you think she ended up linking with Remi?" I asked, trying not to show too much emotion.

"Nah, nigga. She was in that bitch making mad dough, but that nigga Kalel be at a lot of Remi's parties, so he probably put her on." He chuckled.

"Doing what?" I was now interested in what he was actually saying to me.

"Oh, you ain't know she was dancing?"

"Nah, I ain't know that. We don't really kick it like that no more. You know, ever since she got with Kalel." I hung my head.

I couldn't lie, I missed the fuck outta Alex. Bianca had been keeping my attention though, so just as quickly as

Alex would pop in my head, I would push her out.

"Damn nigga, you let that wack ass nigga take yo girl dog!" Rock said clowning me.

"Alex is doing her own thing regardless of how I feel about her. Besides, I'm with Bianca now and shit is smooth. She is a really dope girlfriend," I told him honestly.

"I'm happy for you my nigga. Hold on to that shit. Chicks like her don't come around all the time."

I felt where he was coming from, but I didn't really want to dig in the conversation too much because even though I was rocking with Bianca, Alex was a thing for me and I knew that I would never be able to give Bianca everything as long as shit with me and Alex stayed the way it was.

"Thanks, man."

Rock stood up as if he was about to leave. He reached out to slap me five just as his phone buzzed in his hand.

"Shit let me get up outta here. I'mma take care of that room shit for you my nigga. Don't even worry about it. I'll call you with all the info," Rock said as he walked out of the door, closing it behind him.

His mom was always looking to the next nigga that could take care of her, so being a mother to Rock was not really something she gave a fuck about. She would always say that a boy had to learn how to be a man, and who could teach him better than the streets? I have no idea who came up with her logic, but my mother was nothing like that and it wasn't my place to judge anyone. I went out and sat on the porch, pulling my phone out to call Bianca.

"Hey baby," She cooed answering the phone.

"What's up pretty girl? You got plans for Valentine's Day?" I asked, being funny.

"Not if you didn't make any," Bianca spat at me.

"Relax. You know I got you. I'mma get you some liquor store candies and a rose," I laughed.

She laughed in return. "You couldn't even say that shit with a straight face."

"Damn, you heard that?"

"Yeah I heard that. What are you doing other than being crazy?" She asked.

"Shit, chilling on the porch. What are you doing?" I heard the noise pick up in her background.

"At the grocery store with my Granny, I miss you," Bianca practically whispered.

"I miss you too. Why are you whispering? Is that supposed to be your sexy voice?" I asked, chuckling.

"No this is not my sexy voice silly, I just don't want everybody in the grocery store to hear my conversation. If you don't mind." I could tell she was probably smiling on the other end of the phone.

"Iight, if you say so. I ain't really want shit, just thinking about you. I guess I'll see you when you get here."

"Okay smartass see you soon." She ended the call.

Bianca brought out the joy in me that probably would have died if she didn't come around when she did. With everything that was going on with my mom and Alex disappearing, and then I find out she's dancing at parties. Her grandmother passing was a lot, but Bianca could always put a smile on my face. The saddest part was I still wanted Alex and seeing Rock and hearing the shit that was going on only made it worse.

I sat there with my phone in my hand, debating if I should text Alex or not. I just wanted to know that she was really alright. I figured what the hell, the worse that she could do was not respond.

> Me: *Hey, just want to know you are okay. If this is*
> *still your number.*

I sent the message and dropped my phone in my lap as I watched the people come and go in the projects. When my phone buzzed, I would have never thought that it would be Alex responding, so I was pretty surprised when I saw the message.

> Alex: *Hey, I am fine, taking care of myself. This is*

*not safe so after this, I am changing my number and we will*
*not be able to talk again. I'm sorry.*

I exhaled loudly as I finished the message. This shit with Kalel was starting to piss me off. I thought that if I showed her that I wasn't worried about that wack ass nigga, she would cut me some slack. It seemed like all it did was make her push me away more. I checked the time, as I knew it was coming up on time for me to go see my mother. I tried to go and check on her every day, but my life didn't always allow that with work and everything else.

It was noon. I still had about an hour before I went to see her, so I went back to the house and laid on the couch. I figured I could catch a quick power nap then go and see my mother. Just as I was dozing off, my phone started to buzz loudly in the room.

"Hello," I said grumpily.

"What's up nigga? The room number is 458 and it's for the whole weekend you can get the keys from the desk just give them my name. Enjoy my nigga," Rock damn near shouted into the phone.

"Thanks, man, that shit dope as fuck," I replied, rubbing my eyes.

"Iight, nigga. I'll hit you up later," Rock said before the line went dead.

I laid back down and tried to doze off again. After

about twenty minutes of lying there with my eyes closed, I was out.

***

I wasn't sure what woke me up. I looked at the time and it was just minutes before I had to walk out of the door. I got up and went into the bathroom to wash my face and wake myself all the way up. I came out, grabbed my coat and just as I was opening the door, Bianca was coming up on the porch.

"Hey, you. I knew you were sleeping. I was just coming to wake you up." She kissed me on the cheek.

"Oh shit, I got up just in time. You wanna come? I haven't seen you all day," I asked, locking up the apartment.

"Sure. I don't mind. I haven't seen your mom in a while," Bianca followed me to the car.

I finally looked at her once we were situated.

"You look nice today," I said, starting up the car and backing out of the spot.

"Thank you love bug," She blushed.

We really didn't talk about too much on the ride to the hospital. When we got there, we put everything that we knew we couldn't take in with us in the back seat and headed in. We got to my mother's room and she had been taken for testing for something according to the board on the wall. So,

Bianca and I waited for her in the hallway.

"What's been up with you?" I asked her.

"Nothing much, just helping my Granny get her house together and get her food for the month," She told me in a bubbly tone.

"Ain't you so sweet," I replied, squeezing her cheeks playfully.

"Shut up. You know how I feel about my Granny."

"So, what do you want to do for Valentine's Day?" I asked again, changing the subject.

"Really, I just wanna eat."

I knew that eating was her favorite past time, so I had already had it in my plans to get a good meal. It seemed like I was definitely on the right track with what I had in mind.

"I knew that would be something that you wanted to do," I replied laughing.

The nurse came around the corner with my mother in a wheelchair. Her face lit up the moment she saw us.

"Hey baby boy," Ma said as she rolled past me.

We followed her back into the room as the nurse locked the wheelchair in place and helped her back into bed.

"Hey Bianca, how are you sweetheart?" my mother asked reaching out to her for a hug.

"I'm great, Ms. Setra. How are you today?" Bianca walked over to hug my mother.

"I wanna go home. The food here is horrible," She pulled the cover up on her more.

"What are the doctors saying about that Ma?" I inquired.

"They know for sure that my liver is shit, but now they think it may be something wrong with my heart," Ma hung her head.

"That's not good Ma. How are they going to treat that?" I pulled a chair to her bedside for both me and Bianca to sit down.

"Well I just had a scan for them to look at it. I have to wait to see what that says," she replied, laying her head back on the pillow.

"Well I will be praying for you Ms. Setra," Bianca rubbed her hand.

"Thank you, sweetheart."

"Have you been sleeping?" I asked, worried about her health and if things will look up from here.

"Off and on, but you know they goin fuck with you all night. Shit, I don't see how anybody gets to sleep in a damn hospital," She replied waving her hand as if she was waving it off.

"You can't ask to not be disturbed as much?" I asked.

"I wish I could just tell them to leave me the fuck

alone period," She snapped, making both me and Bianca bust out laughing.

"Ma try not to be mean to these people," I said still laughing.

We sat with my mother for a couple of hours, until she fell asleep on us and we left. We stopped at a little pizza spot close to the house and then back to the apartment. Bianca grabbed the drinks and I carried the pizza, unlocking the door with one hand and letting her in first. I followed closely locking the doors behind me. Bianca flopped down on the couch grabbing the remote off the table and turning on the tv to find a movie.

I sat the pizza on the coffee table and then went into the kitchen to grab some paper plates. When I got back to the living room, *Plug Love* was playing on the tv.

"You like this movie?" I asked laughing.

"Yes, I do actually," Bianca answered sarcastically.

"That's funny," I replied, realizing how hood Bianca could be at times.

"You forgot I was a project chick?" She opened the pizza. She put a piece on a plate and handed it to me.

"I don't think you would ever let me forget that," I replied, laughing as well.

"You damn right."

We watched the movie and ate our pizza. It was dope

as hell, no tension or worries of the outside world, just me and her.

"I love you, Anthony," Bianca blurted out.

I had to tell myself that she had actually said what she said. At first, I didn't know what to say but when she sat up and looked at me, I knew I had to say something.

"Uh, I mean I don't think I'm ready to say that," I told her truthfully.

"Mm, I can respect that, but is it because of Alex?" She asked, looking me in the eyes.

"I mean I wouldn't say it was just that alone, but it does have something to do with it." I replied, hanging my head. I knew I was hurting her with my words, but I couldn't lie to her.

"I know how you feel about her. I saw how you looked at her and how you cared for her. Just don't break my heart for a girl that is treating you like you don't exist," she said and then kissed me on the lips for the first time.

The kiss was so passionate that when she pulled back, I pulled her back in for more. One thing led to another and the next thing I knew, we were on our way to my bedroom. My mother had always been on my head about having condoms with me all the time, so I knew I had the green light to let this happen. I sat Bianca on the bed, gently pulling her shirt up over her head as she undid my belt, dropping my pants to my ankles. I stepped out of them and stepped back as she slid out of hers.

She laid back on the bed, showing off her body in her matching purple panty and bra set. I couldn't lie; for her to be young, she had the body of a woman and that shit had my manhood standing straight up and because it was my first time doing anything like this. I wasn't the pushy type of guy and she hadn't said anything about it, so I didn't bring it up either, but we ended up here anyway. It was time to put in work.

I started kissing and licking her stomach. Just as I was about to slide her panties down, her phone started to ring. I guess from the ringtone she knew something was up. She jumped up and grabbed her pants then snatched her phone from the pocket and answered it. Her face told me something bad was going on she told the person on the other end that she was on her way.

"Anthony I am so sorry, but I have to go. Something is wrong with my grandmother," She said, putting her clothes on in a hurry and rushing out of the room, leaving me there hard as a rock and looking stupid.

When everything finally registered, I jumped up and followed her to the door. She turned around and kissed me before she walked out.

"Call me later and let me know if everything is okay," I called out after her.

"I will," She replied bouncing down the porch steps.

I closed the door and locked it walking back into the bedroom to get my pants. Like any man would be I was pissed shit got cut short like that, but I understood that she had to check on her grandmother. I eventually got over it when I thought about the fact that Valentine's Day was in three days and I knew she was going to be with me that night. So, it would most likely happen that night, so I beat my shit and got it over it.

# ALEX

My phone had been going off like crazy the entire time that I had been asleep. I grabbed it and felt the bed to see if Kalel was still laying next to me. When I realized that he wasn't, I sat up in the bed. He had left me a wad of money on the little stand next to the bed with a note sitting on top of it.

*Go shopping, there is more where that came from.*

*P.S. Look in your purse.*

*-K*

I smiled as I sat the note back down on the stand. I got up looking around the room for my purse. I found it sitting on the dresser. I grabbed it looking inside see what Kalel had left for me. My mouth began to water when I saw the huge sack of powder that was sitting before me, as well as the sack of weed that was tied to it. I looked over at the wraps that he had left for me on the dresser as well.

I grabbed all of it and went back to the bed, using the little stand to roll up. I lit the blunt and hit it like I hadn't smoked in years. I laid back in the bed, thinking of all the money that I made just shaking my ass. It was like once I had done it, a fire started in me. I wanted the best of everything and if I could keep this shit up, I would be set forever.

I heard the front door open. Kalel came in the room

and laid across the bed.

"Hey, I got a job for you. Put something on and come in the living room," Kalel said getting up off of the bed and walking out of the bedroom.

I got up and threw on some shorts and a tank top, not thinking anything of it. When I walked into the living room, it was three other guys sitting on the couch.

"Kalel, what's up?" I asked, confused.

"You wanna make some money, right?" He asked laying his head back on the couch.

"Yeah, you know I'm always game to make money," I replied hesitantly looking around at the other guys.

"Come suck my dick." He caught me off guard.

"What?" I was starting to get uncomfortable.

"Come suck my dick, bitch! You heard me," He shouted, making me jump.

I was scared that he would hit me again, so I dropped to my knees in front of him unbuckled his belt and pulled his dick out. I started to suck it. I could tell he was higher than normal because he was hard before I even touched him for real.

"Oh shit, that's what the fuck I'm talking about," Kalel moaned as I sucked him off as if my life depended on it.

"Damn nigga let me get some of that. How much?" One of the other guys said to Kalel.

"$100 and you got it," Kalel replied.

I thought it was a joke at first. It was bad enough he had me sucking his dick in front of his friends. Now he was selling me like I was some kind of hoe.

"I tell you what. $500 and y'all can get her as a group," Kalel said, changing the odds.

"Shit I got $500 right now, that's nothing," the guy replied, pulling the money out of his pocket.

My heart dropped to my stomach. I didn't know what I was going to do. I just knew that I didn't want to be gang-raped by his friends, but I knew that I wasn't getting out of this. In Kalel's eyes, I owed him and no matter how much money I made him, he was going to hold that over my head until they put me in the ground.

"Go clean yourself up and meet these gentlemen in the bedroom," Kalel said, looking at me with a straight face as he put the money in his pocket.

"Kalel I can't do this," I said in an attempt to change his mind.

He looked at me for a moment before he backhanded me so hard that I flew over the table that was in the living room. Nobody said anything or tried to help me like I knew they wouldn't.

"Now go get cleaned up like I said," he spat at me.

I got up hoping that he didn't hit me again. I made my way to the bathroom. When I looked in the mirror, I saw that my lip was busted, and I had a mark on one of my shoulders. I let the few little tears that forced their way out on my face then I wiped them away. In the process, I took a quick bump from the coke tray that Kalel kept in the bathroom, cleaning myself up and getting as high as I could while doing it.

I figured if I had to live this life, I was going to do it high as a fucking giraffe's pussy because I was going to lose it otherwise. I sprayed on some perfume and pulled my hair up. I came back out of the bathroom and walked into the bedroom. I laid down in the bed and closed my eyes as the tears welled up in them.

I heard the footsteps coming into the bedroom. My heart started to pound in my chest. I knew that this moment would change me forever, but there was nothing I could do about it if I didn't want to be on the streets. I had left everything that ever loved and cared about me behind and now it was time to make grown woman decisions. The first guy climbed up on the bed, shaking me from my thoughts and making me face reality.

He opened my legs slowly as he positioned himself to invade my personal space. Pulling my shorts off and throwing them on the floor, he rubbed his fingers against my love button. I gasped in disgust, but I said nothing.

"Damn dis shit wet as fuck girl," He breathed into my ear as he rammed himself inside me.

I laid there, letting him have his way with me, wishing that I could just step out of my body and be somewhere else. After a few pumps, I went numb. The only thing I could do was lay there lifelessly, thinking about how Anthony would have never let anything like this happen to me, let alone set it up. Kalel didn't love me, he loved what I could make happen for him. To him, I meant nothing more than the $500 that he received for pimping out my pussy.

By the time that I came back to reality, the other guys had their turns and the last one was coming up to bat. I just kept telling myself that it was almost over when I felt the smooth quick pumper starting to shake on top of me. I knew his end was going to be sooner than later. When he slid his limp dick out of me, I rolled over and balled up as they all walked out of the bedroom laughing, fixing their clothes.

When I heard the front door close and I didn't hear voices in the living room anymore, I got up and went into the bathroom to clean myself up from the mess that was made on top of me. I peeled my cum infested shirt over my head and turned the shower on all hot water. I got in immediately. I felt like a bucket of shit standing in that shower. I still couldn't believe that Kalel would put me through something like that. I knew that his power trip wasn't over by a long shot.

I stood there as the tears poured out of me like someone had flipped a switch on in the back of my head or something. I scrubbed my body like I would get new skin if I scrubbed off what I had already. I finished up my shower and grabbed my towel, wrapping it around my body. I stepped out and looked in the bathroom mirror. Standing there, I stared at my reflection. I was there, staring at someone that I had never seen before in my life. I had dark circles around my eyes and the hurt that I had just endured pooled in my expression.

I looked at the mound of Cocaine on the tray that Kalel had left behind. Still wrapped in my towel, I grabbed the tray and went back into the bedroom. I sat in the middle of the bed and started sniffing as much as I could. The burning in my nose felt like I was putting lighters up to it. The tears started running again as I kept snorting. The next thing I knew, everything around me started spinning and I was out.

Kalel was slapping my face and calling my name and I was soaking wet and freezing. I opened my eyes to his tears running into my eyes, and the shower running on my face.

"Alex! Oh my god! I thought I had lost you!" He

shouted, pulling me into him.

"What happened?" I asked confused.

"You damn near overdosed! What the fuck were you thinking?" He jumped up from out of the tub as his emotions of fear quickly changed to anger.

"Overdosed?" I asked, trying to remember everything that happened.

"Yes, Alex, overdose! What the fuck were you thinking about?" He snapped at me again.

"Honestly, I was thinking about you selling my pussy for $500," I told him honestly. I was over his shit. While I was sitting and preparing myself for what I now know was an overdose, I decided that if I had to stay with him and deal with his shit that I was going to give him everything he gave me from this moment forward.

He looked at me like my head had just done a 360 on my shoulders.

"That was business, you know that," He replied looking dumb.

"For who? I don't remember saying I wanted to be a part of that business!"

"Alex, do not bitch up on me now."

"Fuck that and fuck you!" I replied attempting to get out of the tub.

Kalel lunged at me, grabbing me up from the collar of

my shirt as if he was going to hit me. I looked up at him with the straightest face, stopping him in his tracks.

"Go ahead," I replied, taunting him. It really wasn't anything else that he could do to me that would hurt worse than what he had already done.

He looked at me for a minute. I could see the wheels turning in his head as to what he would do to me next. He finally dropped me back into the tub and walked out of the apartment. I pulled myself up out of the tub and made my way back to the bedroom. I groped the wall as I made my way to my bag to find something fresh to wear. I pulled out a long T-shirt and some panties. I barely made it to the bed before my energy depleted.

I was able to put my panties on while lying there, but I had to wait if I was going to put my shirt on. I stared out of the window over the bed at the night sky thanking god that I was even able to see it again. I wasn't trying to kill myself, I just wanted the pain and disgust to go away. I listened to my heartbeat slowing in rhythm as my breathing started to calm itself.

I sat up, pulling my shirt over my head. I grabbed my phone from the dresser and went to Anthony's contact information. I hit the send button before I even thought about it. It rang twice and then a female picked up the phone. I listened to the person say hello a few times and I could have sworn I knew the voice. I hung up quickly, tossing my phone across the bed.

I stood up hoping that my legs would work for me and headed into the kitchen to try and find something to put on my stomach. I moved like a slug all the way to the fridge, praying that god just kept me on my feet. I was finally able to make myself a sandwich and get my belly right. I stood right there in the kitchen and ate. When I was done, I had a nice cold glass of tap water and went back to bed.

I curled up under the blanket, thinking about the female voice that answered Anthony's phone and trying to force myself to sleep. I told myself that he had just gotten his number changed. I mean, I did tell him I could never talk to him again after my boyfriend shot him in the shoulder. Then the fact that he may have had a girlfriend rolled around in my head. That had my stomach fucked up; the thing that really had me fucked up was in the back of mind, I knew that the female voice was Bianca.

*** 

The next afternoon my phone buzzed, alerting me that I had a message. I picked it up and looked to see who the message was from. I was shocked to see that it was from Anthony.

*Anthony: Hey, I just want to know you are okay. If*

*this is still your number.*

I read the message thinking of the irony of him texting me after the night before. I thought that it would be best to close this chapter of my life for good. I mean we were both in relationships and there was never anything between us, so what did I have to lose? I exhaled softly before I replied.

*Me: Hey, I am fine, taking care of myself. This is not safe so after this, I am changing my number and we will not be able to talk again. I'm sorry.*

I closed my eyes and let out a sigh. I brought his contact info back up and blocked and deleted his number. I figured he had moved on so he wasn't really thinking about me and he probably wouldn't even notice. I tossed my phone on the bed and looked over at the cocaine tray that was completely empty now. I figured Kalel had cleared it out, so I didn't have another mishap. I got up and went to my purse to see if I still had my stash. I was overjoyed when I saw that I still had something.

I rolled up a blunt and laid in the bed, getting as high as I could before Kalel came back. I hated him for what he did to me, but I was grateful at the same time because he had unleashed the savage in me. I'd made it up in my mind that the moment I got away from him, I was going to take everything he ever owned and loved, then I was goin kill his bitch ass!

# ANTHONY

*Valentine's Day...*

The time had come for me to pull off my big surprise for Bianca. I had gone to the hotel to get everything set up, at first the front desk agent was giving me a hard time. The I remembered what Rock told me on the phone, once I said his name she asked for my ID and the key was in my hand. When I walked in my jaw hit the floor. This was the most beautiful suite I had ever seen, and I knew that Bianca would love it. I made sure that it was condoms in the nightstand just in case shit got real. I spread the rose petals around on the bed and floor and in the bathroom and got everything looking all romantic. After sitting all the gifts that I had got her on the bed, I slid the light switch down just enough to set the mood.

Once I had everything set up right, I headed back to the apartment to wait for Bianca. When I pulled up in the parking lot I noticed that she was sitting on the porch reading a book. I parked the truck and got out.

"Waiting on someone?" I asked smiling widely.

"Oh yeah, my boyfriend should be here any minute now," She replied playing my game and smiling back at me.

"Aww snap. You have a boyfriend? That sucks. I was

hoping I had a chance." I kissed her on the forehead and walked past her to unlock the door.

"Happy Valentine's Day, baby," Bianca said as she grabbed my hand and walked with me into the apartment.

"Happy Valentine's Day." I stepped back out to pull the mail out of the mailbox and closed the door behind me when I came back in.

"So, where is my gift?" Bianca asked with a confused look on her face.

"You will get them, it's just going to be later," I chuckled at the look on her face.

"So, that means its more than one?" She inquired smiling hard.

"Maybe, maybe not," I grabbed the remote as I sat down on the couch.

"You are an asshole sometimes." Bianca flopped down next to me.

"Sometimes," I replied pulling her into me to snuggle her.

She snuggled under me and we got sucked into some movie that was on the Bounce channel.

I set my alarm so that we wouldn't miss our dinner reservations at the restaurant in the hotel. I knew that I was limited to the things I could do because of my age, but there was nothing I could do about that right at the moment. By the time it went off, Bianca had fallen asleep on my chest.

"B, we gotta go, baby," I said trying to wake her.

"Okay, just give me a few more minutes."

"We gotta go. We're going to miss our reservation," I told her, laughing at her cute unawareness.

"Ugh, okay let's go," she said, finally sitting up and grabbing her shoes.

She hated being woke up and I knew it but if I wanted my plans to work, we had to get out of the door. We both got our shit on and were in the truck in no time. Once Bianca was in her seatbelt, she drifted right back off. I chuckled to myself watching her get comfortable in the seat.

I rode silently, praying that everything worked out the way I needed it to go. I had put a lot of hard work in for this night and I would be pissed the fuck off if something went wrong. I wanted tonight to be a symbol of my appreciation for everything that Bianca had done for me since we had started talking and how she always made sure to keep me on my toes.

We finally pulled into the hotel parking garage. I parked the truck on the first level.

"B, we here. Wake up," I said shaking her softly to pull her from her peaceful slumber.

"I'm up," She replied groggily, sitting up and

grabbing her purse.

"Come on, I'll carry something if you need me to," I grabbed my bag out of the backseat.

"Where are we?" She asked, finally waking up and looking around.

"The Motor City Hotel," I grinned.

"Are you for real?" Her face lit up.

"Yes, we have reservations for dinner," I replied candidly.

"Aww baby, this is dope as fuck!"

I grabbed everything that I needed and got out of the truck. I walked around to her side and opened her door, helping her down. We walked hand and hand into the hotel. I wasn't ready to show her the room yet so I asked the agent at the desk if she could watch our bags when Bianca stepped from the desk to look around the lobby.

Once I had the keys, we headed to the restaurant for dinner, when we walked in I told the host my name and he showed us to the table. I pulled out Bianca's chair waiting for her to sit down. I then went to my seat across from her. The atmosphere in the restaurant was really romantic and it had just so happened that they had a Valentine's Day dinner special.

We both ended up with lobster tails and garlic mashed potatoes with steamed broccoli. Bianca ordered a virgin daiquiri for her drink and I had a regular coke.

"Anthony, this is beautiful. No one has ever done anything like this for me before," Bianca cooed across the table.

"There's more," I told her, shoving a forkful of food in my mouth.

"Stop playing with me, "she said, full of excitement.

"There is," I replied smiling. I couldn't lie. I felt all the way like the man, and I knew that Bianca was going to have a great evening and she didn't even know what was about to hit her.

We finished our meal, laughing and talking, kicking the shit, then it was time to go up to the room. I started to get nervous as we got on the elevators. I just wanted everything to go right.

"We got a room, too?" Bianca asked, wondering why we were getting on the elevator.

"Yes, we got a room too," I replied laughing.

I thought it was cute that she was so excited. I mean I knew that we came from the same hood and usually we didn't get to do shit like this, but she was really excited. It showed me how wack those dope niggas really were. They were making all this money and couldn't even take they chick out on a real date.

The elevators opened up to the beautiful hallway and Bianca's eyes lit up even more. I stepped out of the elevator, putting arms in front of the door to hold them open for her, pointing her in the direction of our room.

I watched her as she skipped down the hallway. She started to slow up as we got towards the end. I stopped at our room door and pulled out the key, opening the door and allowing Bianca to walk in first. The timer that I had put on the small speaker that I brought worked out perfectly as the music softly serenaded the entire room as we walked in.

"Aww baby, this is so beautiful," Bianca said turned to hug me.

"Happy Valentine's Day pretty girl," I replied kissing her on the lips.

She walked over to the bed where I had laid a dozen roses out for her picking them up and smelling them. She walked around the room admiring all of my hard work. I had all types of shit for her: Pink outfits, money, anything that I could think that she would want.

I went into the bathroom and started the water in the whirlpool tub. I had put all the fragrance stuff in the tub before I left. I pulled the two shower robes from the closet and laid them on the chairs that sat next to the bed.

"Why don't we take a nice hot bath together and unwind on this beautiful Valentine's night," I suggested, wrapping my arms around her waist from behind.

"Oh, a bath sounds good." Bianca stepped over to one of the chairs taking her purse off and sitting it in the chair.

She followed up with her shirt until she was completely naked standing before me. I was so sucked into her body and how beautiful she really was that I didn't even notice that I hadn't taken anything off until she turned around to look at me.

"Why are you still dressed?" She said with a sexy giggle.

"Oh shit, you had me stuck for a minute," I replied rubbing my forehead.

I took all my stuff off and laid it in the other chair, I went back into the bathroom and turned the water off in the tub. As I was doing that Bianca stepped into the tub letting out a low moan as the hot water caressed her skin.

"Damn, sound like you got the party started without me." I had never done anything like this before.

"Nah, this water just hot as fuck," She replied laughing.

"I thought girls liked they water on 'cook a nigga'," I laughed as well.

"Probably not when we gotta sit in it, maybe a shower." Bianca moved to turn on some cold water as I stepped in, understating what she was talking about.

"Oh shit, my bad this shit is hot as fuck," I laughed awkwardly.

"See I told you," She replied laughing at me as I tried to dip my balls in the water to test and see if I could actually sit down.

"Okay peanut gallery, while you're worried about me, this water goin be ice cold," I shot at her, finally able to sit down.

She turned off the water and moved closer to me so I could put my arm around her as we relaxed in the warm water.

"This is so sweet Anthony. I have never had anyone care enough about me to put this much thought into something so romantic. Thank you," Bianca said laying her head back on me.

For a split second, I thought I had lost my mind because when I looked over at the mirror I could have sworn that I was holding Alex instead of Bianca. I instantly started to feel like shit. Here I was in a nice hotel suite with Bianca for Valentine's Day, thinking about Alex.

"Anthony, did you hear me?" Bianca asked snatching me out of my fuckery.

"Oh yeah, I'm good, and you are more than welcome. You deserve it," I replied kissing her on the ear.

"Who taught you how to be so romantic?" She asked turning to look me in my face.

"Well, my pops always did stuff like this for my mom and I always said that if I got a girl that I felt like was worth it, I would do it for her."

"Well, your pops was a wonderful man and I am sure he made your mother very happy doing these things, just like you have made me happy and given me the best Valentine's Day I have ever had," She kissed my lips passionately.

I kissed her back, thinking about our close call a couple of days before. In my head, I was hoping that after all this work that we could finally go all the way and from the looks of things, my dreams were about to come true even though it wasn't with the person that I had expected.

"Let's get cleaned up so we can finish what we started the other day," Bianca said giving me what I assumed to be bedroom eyes. She was definitely ready to go the way she was stroking my meat under the water while we were kissing.

"I'm game for that," I replied grabbing the soft sponge that I had brought earlier just for this occasion.

We washed each other's bodies and let the water out headed to the bed. Luckily the playlist that I had made for the night was 24 hours long so we wouldn't be running out of music anytime soon. When we got back to the bed, Time by Sebastian Mikael was playing. It was like the Valentine gods were working in my favor.

"You want me to lay down? "She asked looking for me to take control.

I really didn't know what to do from here. I just knew what I wanted to do, so I let my imagination take control.

"Yeah lay down," I replied walking over to the nightstand and grabbing a condom tearing it open as Bianca slid her naked body under the covers.

I rolled the condom down on my meat stick and slid between the covers with her. The time was finally here and so far everything had worked out great. She climbed on top of me.

"Have you ever done this before?" She asked shyly.

"Nah, not for real," I replied honestly.

Bianca giggled nervously. "Well that's good. Neither have I, now I don't feel so bad."

"That helps a lot, here you lay down and I will get on top then," I replied feeling stupid for not knowing what to do next.

We switched places and that's when shit got real. The moment my dick touched her body, I could have exploded everywhere but I was determined to leave this night with my dignity at least. I lined myself up with her love hole and started the process of getting inside her tight walls.

"Ouch," she whispered biting her bottom lip.

"My bad, you want me to stop?" I asked not trying to hurt her or make her uncomfortable.

"Nah, it just a little more painful then I thought it would be." She took a deep breath, ready for whatever was to come next.

"I can go slower and be a little gentler," I eased up a little.

That was one thing my dad did get to talk to me about before he passed. He told me when it was time for me to have sex for the first time there were two things that I should always remember. Never be too rough; pussy is like a delicate flower, and the second thing was jackhammer is not attractive. My stroke needed to be strong and steady.

"Here put it right here." She placed me in the right position.

I took her help and got my shit together. I felt when the tip started to slide inside of her.

"Mm, Anthony," she cried out grabbing onto my arms.

"Shit, this is crazy," I blurted, starting to understand what the big fuss about pussy really was.

Finally, I broke through and I was in there. I

remembered to keep my stroke strong and steady, but the tightness of her walls and how wet and warm they were was really making it hard to concentrate.

"Mm, I didn't know it would feel this good," Bianca whispered in my ear.

"Shit neither did I," I replied still trying to focus so I didn't come too quick.

We were going good and everything was great until I felt the nut building up in the tip of my dick. I knew I didn't have much longer to go, but I was going to make the best of it while I still had it in me.

"Oh shit, I think I'mma cum," Bianca cried out as her pussy started to create water like no other. The shit was everywhere and that was all I needed before my finale had come and gone.

I rolled back over to what I guess I could consider my side of the bed and lifted the cover to look at the damage that was done, and that's when I saw it. The condom was gone. I knew that I had put one on, but that bitch was nowhere to be found when it was all said and done. My heart started pounding because I knew what could happen. I laid there, praying that God would have mercy on me, so my mother didn't have to kill me.

"What's wrong, was it me?" Bianca asked. I assumed she could see the emotion change in my face.

"The condom broke, Bianca," I blurted out.

It didn't make sense to not tell her. We were in this shit together at this point.

"What do you mean it broke?" I could hear the panic riding her voice.

"I just looked down at my dick, the condom wasn't on it anymore," I replied in just as much panic as she was.

Without any words, she kissed me on the lips and laid on my chest. I didn't say another word about it. I was scared as hell, but I didn't want to ruin the night for her or myself, really. I had just had sex for the first time and although I wanted like hell for it to be with Alex, Bianca wasn't all that bad. I just knew that if she did get pregnant it was because of that squirting shit and if we kept fucking and she kept doing that shit, I was going to keep bussin like that. Eventually, we both fell asleep and we were headed to a new day with new shit to deal with.

# ALEX

I laid in the bed listening to Kalel snore, which was something he only did after he had been out getting high and partying for days. I stared out of the window looking at the stars and the only thing that I could think about was Anthony. I just wondered if he thought about me as I thought about him. I thought about all the times he tried to shoot his shot and I turned him down, wanting him to be more like the dope boys. Now, look at me, stuck with a bum ass dope boy that was pretty much holding me hostage.

He was my only hope in the world. I just missed being able to talk to someone that actually used their brain. I couldn't sit and talk to Kalel about my dreams and ambitions or my goals in life. His dumbass would probably think I was trying to leave him. I missed my friend that was always there for me. I felt bad for the way things happened. I knew that when I got away from Kalel I was going to mend my relationship with Anthony. I had to; my life would never be right if I didn't fix shit between us.

I just kept thinking about that girl that answered the phone. It just made me wonder. I looked over at my phone on the little stand by the bed for a moment before I grabbed it. I sat up, sliding out of the bed slowly trying not to wake Kalel.

I tiptoed into the bathroom closing the door behind me. I pulled up Anthony's contact and I hit the call button. The phone rang so loudly in my ear that it made me jump. I paced back and forth as I waited for someone to answer.

"Hello." A female voice came through the phone.

"Um, hi, I was looking for someone named Anthony," I said in almost a whisper.

"Who is this?" The voice spat.

"Um, I'm his friend, Alex," I replied confused.

"Alex this is Bianca. You don't know my voice?" She snapped as if I was supposed to know it was her.

"Bianca, where is Anthony?" I asked thinking nothing of it.

"I'm sorry, my boyfriend is not going to be able to talk to you, boo. We chilling. Maybe he can call you back another day."

"What the fuck..." was all I could get out before the line went dead.

I couldn't fucking believe that Anthony and Bianca had gotten together. I always knew he was playing a role when he would talk shit about her when we all kicked it together. I felt my eyes start to burn, but I couldn't let myself cry. I took a couple of deep breaths, got my shit together and went to get back in the bed. I sat my phone back on the stand then I slid back under the cover.

"You do that shit again and I'm goin' break your fuckin jaw," Kalel spoke, rolling over and pulling the cover over him.

I couldn't even say anything, I just looked at him. I was shocked that he heard me all the way in the bathroom. I turned over and laid down as the barriers broke and the tears were set free. I didn't know what I had done, but I was convinced that Kalel was my karma for something. I laid there, holding myself and crying until my eyelids got too heavy to hold open.

***

I didn't wake up until the next afternoon. I assumed that my body was tired from all the late nights and decided that it was going to take its beauty rest because I felt like new money when I got up. The apartment was quiet, so I assumed that Kalel was gone, but I got up and looked around the apartment just to be sure. Hell, he could have been in the living room auctioning off my goods again. Once I saw the coast was clear, I went into the bathroom and got myself together.

When I came back into the room, I grabbed my phone started checking my notifications. The first thing that popped up was a text message from Anthony.

Anthony: *Sorry about last night.*

My blood boiled. Of all the things that he could have said, all he chose to say was *"Sorry about last night"?* He couldn't be serious. I had to keep my cool and play my role and make it seem like it wasn't a big deal.

*Me: Oh, it's cool I am happy for you guys...*

I lied. I knew I couldn't tell him how I really felt because I was with Kalel and I couldn't do anything about it. I just didn't feel like she was good enough for him. Anthony was a sweet and romantic guy with a big heart and any woman could see that his momma raised him right. Bianca, on the other hand, was a rachet ass, bald head ass, project rat ass bitch. I hated the thought of her touching and being intimate with him. I knew that no matter how mad I was about them being together, I couldn't be mad at anyone but myself. I was so caught up in the fast life that I forgot about how good the simple things could be. I put my phone down and slid my hand under my pillow, grabbing my stash. I fed both nostrils a little bump and eventually shit didn't even matter anymore.

I was learning the hard way, that I could have my cake and eat it too. I couldn't flash Kalel all in Anthony's face and expect him not to get fed up with my shit at some point. I was snatched out of my head when heard the front door close loudly. I knew just by the way that Kalel came into the apartment that it was going to be some shit, especially when he came storming in the bedroom throwing shit.

"This is some bullshit!" he shouted, flinging his jacket on the bed.

"What's wrong?" I asked, looking at him like he was crazy.

"We don't have any more money and Remi just called me and told me that the after-hours spot got raided last night. The night before your next big party now we don't have an income," he snapped holding his head.

I for damn sure wasn't going to tell him that I still had all the money that he put on the stand for me. I figured I could just make that my rainy-day fund since I was trying to get away from him as soon as possible, anyway.

"Can I just go dance in the clubs?" I asked, throwing out suggestions so he didn't start taking his anger out on me as usual.

"You're not old enough to get a dancing license, and there aren't any clubs that are willing to let you dance 'cause they ain't trying to get shut down. You goin' have to start sucking some more dicks around this muthafucka," Kalel casually said as he entered the bathroom.

It was really mind-boggling that he felt like he could sell my pussy anytime he wanted to. That shit was beyond me, but like always, I knew it was nothing I could do about it if I didn't want to have to fight my way out.

"Are there any more after-hours that will let me dance?" I called out to him. At this point, I was only worried about myself and making more money to pull off my plan.

"I'm waiting for Remi to call me back and let me know what's up. She was talking about having it at her and Deon's, but that shit too hot" He came back into the bedroom, sitting on the foot of the bed to roll a blunt.

"We can get through this," I replied, trying to diffuse the situation that I could see brewing.

Kalel was all about his money and when he couldn't get it the way he wanted it, shit got real bad, real quick. So, I knew that if I didn't want to become his punching bag that I needed to get him out of his funk before he found a way to blame me for all the bad shit that was happening in his life.

"I just need to find a girl that is older than you so when we get in droughts like this, both of yall can be bringing in money." He lit the blunt in his hand.

That idea wasn't all that bad when I sat back and thought about it in hindsight. If there was another girl here to keep his attention, I could make my escape and he wouldn't even notice. I had to take advantage of that for sure.

"So, do you want me to find another girl?" I asked

hoping the answer was yes.

"I already got some shit on the floor, we were supposed to meet her at the party tomorrow night, but that shit looking like it ain't goin' happen," he replied taking a long hit from the blunt before passing it to me.

"It will all working out," I replied, taking the blunt from him and taking a long drag from it.

I sat back on the bed, enjoying the opening for an opportunity as I started to build my master plan of getting my life back on track. We were just getting into the second blunt when his phone started to ring in his pocket. Kalel hurried to get it out of his pocket and see who it was. It must have been the call he was waiting for because when he looked at his phone, he jumped up and walked into the living room.

I wasn't really in the mood to ear hustle, so I just let it be. It wasn't anything that was done that wouldn't come out eventually anyway. I was just about to snuggle back under the covers when Kalel came back in the bedroom.

"Get dressed, we got money to make. I will be back to get you in an hour." He grabbed something from the closet and headed back out of the bedroom and out of the front door.

I got up and grabbed my bags to find something to wear before going to wash my ass. I was ready in less than an hour but that gave me time to get my nerves under control.

Kalel had been on so much wild shit lately I didn't know how to feel about having money to make because I didn't know what was included in the deal. Hell, he could be trying to sell me for all I knew. I thought back to how the shots that Remi had given me at my first party and how the liquor mellowed me out. I walked out into the living room where Kalel had built himself a mini bar in search of something that could help me.

I finally came across a small bottle of Hennessey. I unscrewed the top and put the bottle to my lips, throwing it back quickly once or twice. I put the top back on the bottle and put it back where I got it from. I had made my move just in the nick of time because just as I was walking away from the bar, Kalel walked in the door.

"Hey, you ready to go get this money?" He asked, his mood seeming happier than when he left.

"I'm ready. You must have gotten some good news on that phone call," I replied candidly.

"Remi had some really good news for me, but we can talk about that later. We really need to be getting out of here," He replied walking over to the bar and pouring himself a drink.

I folded my lips together hoping that he wasn't going for the Hennessey that I had just dipped into. When I saw him reach for the Brandy instead, I could have jumped for joy. He filled his cup, grabbed his jacket and we headed out. After a rather short drive, we pulled up in front of a house that I had never seen before.

Kalel parked the truck and jumped out without saying a word to me, so instead of sitting there looking stupid, I jumped out and followed him up to the door. He had already knocked by the time I got to him. After a few seconds, I heard Remi's voice getting closer to the door as she opened it.

Without saying anything she stepped to the side, letting us in.

"Hey, Alex boo, what you been up to?" She asked, excited to see me.

"Shit girl you know me, trying to find new ways to get this money," I replied smiling wide happy to see her as well.

"Damn you don't see me?" Kalel spat her.

"Boy, fuck you," Remi snapped back at him reaching for my arm.

"Come on Alex, the ladies are in the basement. Let the men talk business up here." Remi led me to the stairs.

I followed her down the stairs and into what looked like a completely different house.

"So, what's been up? I haven't seen you since the

party." She walked over to the full bar and pulled out two shot glasses.

"It's been a lot of shit going on lately," I sighed, trying not to go into too much detail as I sat down on the couch.

"You sure?" She asked, implying that she knew something I wasn't telling.

"I'm sure," I lied. I didn't want to think about prior events.

"Okay well I won't pry, but I will say this. You are a beautiful girl and you could be doing a million other things with your life," she said without even looking up at me as she poured us both a shot.

"Remi, what are you really trying to say to me?"

"I know what Kalel did to you. That shit is fucked up and you don't have to go through that. You ain't his fucking sex slave. Now where you are right now can be your living space if you want it. It's completely set up to be used as a one-bedroom apartment," she replied, walking over sitting on the couch and handing me one of the shot glasses.

I took the glass from her, dumping the liquid in my mouth and swallowing it down quickly.

"How did you hear about it?" I asked, my face flush from embarrassment.

"Kalel came over here bragging about it the day after it happened."

"Is this you and Deon's house?" I asked.

"Yeah this is where we are most of the time." I could tell that she was wondering why I asked that question from the look on her face.

"I asked because you're offering this space up to me to get away from Kalel, but he can always come here and find me."

"Well, Deon wasn't feeling how he was bragging about doing something like that to you and now he really doesn't want to fuck with him like that. we talked about it this morning, and we can't just leave you in that situation, so we want to get you out then cut him off completely." Remi took a deep breath when she was finished talking as she waited for me to respond.

'So, ya'll are goin to keep me safe?' I asked, seeing my chance to get away open up right before my eyes.

"Actually, my little brother Rock is going to be here. Think of him as your personal bodyguard until we can get this shit figured out."

I sat there taking all of her words in, careful to make sure that my next move was my best move.

"Can I sleep on it?" I asked not really knowing what to say right then.

I mean at the end of the day, I had to remember that these were Kalel's friends before they were mine. Could I really trust them? Could I really call them my friends?

"Yeah, but I need you to think quickly. Shit is about to hit the fan between Kalel and Rock, and I don't want you to be caught up in it," Remi replied with a worried look on her face.

"What are you talking about?" I asked starting to get worried myself.

"Kalel owes some really bad people some money. If he doesn't get them the money soon, they are going to kill him. My brother works for those people. They send him out to collect." Remi got up and went back to the bar to pour another shot for herself.

"So, what does that have to do with me?" I asked, now panicking.

"The people that he owes are very bad people, Alex, and they don't care who they kill if it comes to killing at all. If you hang around him you are just as much a target because they don't know you. They could think that you two were in cahoots."

"Well, like I said, let me sleep on it so I can make the best move and I will hit you up," I replied as we heard the footsteps coming down the stairs.

"Fuck yall down here whispering about?" Deon's voice boomed as he walked over to the couch Kalel was on, and some chick followed behind him.

"Our periods," Remi shot at him sarcastically, trying to change the mood in the room.

"Man get out of here, with that weird-ass shit," Kalel whined covering his ears.

"Boy fuck you. Grow up!" Remi spat at him.

"Alright back to business. I want everyone to meet shay," Deon chimed in, changing the subject.

When I heard the name Shay I knew that I had heard it before, but I figured it could have been a billion bitches in the world name Shay. When I looked up at the girl that was being introduced to me, I felt my heart stop for a second. So much so I grabbed my chest and cleared my throat a little.

"Oh, hey Alex," Shay said looking me dead in the face.

"Hey Shay," I tried hard not to show weakness.

"You two know each other?" Kalel asked, looking confused.

"Yeah, that's Bianca's cousin, Shay. She has been around the hood from time to time, you just weren't around," I replied finally exhaling.

"Well that makes shit a lot easier," Deon replied laughing loudly.

"I guess it does," I replied laying back on the couch.

# ANTHONY

Valentine's Day had changed the whole dynamic of everything about me and Bianca. Shit was starting to feel like a real long-term relationship we had been kicking it for about 2 months. We had started spending more and more time with each other until it was as if she lived in the apartment with me. The doctors were saying that my mother could come home soon, and the bills were starting to back up on me. So, Bianca got a little part-time job and was helping me pay the bills.

Everything in my life was coming together, but I was starting to notice a change in Bianca's attitude and her everyday habits. She was starting to sleep all the time and she was mean as hell at least six of the seven days of the week. We started to argue about dumb shit, and it was getting old real quick. I had found out that Alex called me while I was asleep one night and Bianca answered my phone. I didn't like that sneaky shit at all. The part that was really eating away at me was that I know finding out that I was with Bianca probably hurt Alex and I would have never wanted her to find out that way.

I had just pulled into the parking space from work

when I saw Bianca sitting on the porch. From a distance, she looked like she was sleeping, so my interest was peaked immediately. I jumped out of the truck and headed over to her.

"You good?" I asked, catching her attention as I walked up to the porch.

"That depends on you," she replied, lifting her head revealing the tears running down her face.

"What's going on?" I replied cutting straight to the point as I sat down next to her.

"Anthony, I'm pregnant." Bianca broke out into a loud sob.

Her words echoed in my head as they began to register.

"Pregnant…damn, okay, I got you. I'm going to be a real father. I'm going to hold you and my baby down no matter what," I said out loud, trying to convince myself that I had shit together through the fear that was surging through my body.

"You serious?" Bianca asked, looking up at me with a relieved look on her face.

"Yeah, I laid down and made the baby with you. Now I have to step up and take care of my responsibilities."

I started to think about my pops and what he would

say to me at this moment. I am sure both him and my mother would be very disappointed in me for this, but I also knew that they would expect me to take care of my child. My mother had me young and my father was by her side all the way and then he married her. I was about to have a family, so I knew what I had to do.

I helped Bianca into the apartment, making a second trip for my shit. Once I got her in the bed and snug under the covers so she could get some rest, I grabbed my keys and headed out to go and see my mother to tell her the news. The whole ride to the hospital I rehearsed how I would tell my mother that her 17-year-old son was about to give her a grandchild. I knew she was going to flip out on me, but I did the crime. I was going to have to do the time at some point.

The only thing that I had that could really save me is the fact that I actually had on a condom. I finally pulled in to the hospital parking lot parking close to the door. I threw the truck in park and hopped out damn near speed walking to the desk to get my visitor's card so I could go up to my mother's room. My mind raced as I climbed on the elevator. I said a quick prayer just as I came to my mother's floor and the elevator doors opened.

I walked by the nurses' station casually, wiping away the beads of sweat that were starting to form on my forehead. When I got to my mother's room I stood there for a moment trying to catch my breath. I finally walked into the room, noticing Ma sitting up bright-eyed and bushy-tailed, watching her soap operas.

"Hey baby boy," she said through her smile.

"Hey Ma," I replied hanging my head.

"What's wrong?" She asked, her face turning concerned with a hint of panic.

"I'mma be a daddy, Ma," I replied, closing my eyes so I wouldn't have to see the right hook coming.

Sadness immediately washed over her face. "Anthony, no."

"Ma, I am so sorry. I had a condom on and everything," I replied trying to state my case before she bit my head off.

"Wait, you had on a condom and she still got pregnant?" She asked confused.

"It broke. I put it on before we started and when it was over the condom wasn't there anymore," I replied honestly as I paced back and forth.

"Well, how does she feel about it?" She asked repositioning herself in the hospital bed.

"She thought I was going to leave her," I replied shaking my head at the thought of leaving my child behind.

"Did you reassure her that is not how this family

works?" She asked as tears welled up in her eyes.

"I did, I told her I was going to make sure her and the baby were good no matter what," I replied as tears started to build up in my eyes as well.

My mother reached her hand out for me to come to her. She grabbed my hand as I got closer to her and kissed it.

"You remind me so much of your father. I know you thought I was going to go the hell off in here. At first, I was, but looking at the circumstances this baby was meant to be here. It's just seeing how you are handling it at such a young age warms my heart. We did good," My mother said with tears now running down her face and mine as well.

I certainly was not expecting that, but it was nice to know that even though this was something she fought to keep me from while I was growing up, she was proud that I was stepping up to the plate.

"Thanks, Ma," I replied kissing her hand as well.

"Aww, I'm going to be a grandma. I gotta get the hell out of here," she chuckled.

"That's crazy," I whispered to myself still trying to believe that I was going to be a father.

If someone would have told me that I would end up with Bianca instead of Alex I probably would have punched them out. Shit was moving so fast and all I could do was move accordingly.

"All I ask is no matter what happens between you two just make sure my grandbaby is good. Shit is about to get real and if you don't really love this girl it is going to show. You need to get yourself right; families don't always stay together if you catch my drift," She replied looking up at me.

My mother knew how I felt about Alex, it was just something about her that wouldn't let me shake her even knowing that she was with Kalel.

"I got it Ma, but I need to go take care of some things. I will call and check on you later," I said, kissing her on the cheek and heading out into the hallway.

I pulled my phone out of my pocket as I walked down the hallway calling Rock. He picked up on the first ring.

"What's up my nigga," He belted through the phone.

"Aye, I need to holla at you about something, when will you be free?" I asked as I hurried to the truck.

"Meet me at the Trap in about 15 minutes," He sensed the urgency in my voice.

"Iight, I'm on my way," I replied ending the call.

My life had taken a different turn. It was time for me to man up and start making moves to give my child the best life possible. I jumped in the truck and headed over to see Rock. When I pulled up in front of the house, I saw Rock's truck in the driveway. I shut the car off and sat there for a moment thinking about what I was about to do and if it was the best move to make.

I looked at my current situation and how shit had gotten heavy and I knew it was now or never. I snatched the keys from the ignition and got up the truck walking up to the porch. Before I could ring the bell Rock opened the door letting me inside the house. The house smelled of breakfast and weed smoke, I chuckled as Rock brushed past me in a house robe and house shoes, shuffling his feet like an old man with a bad knee.

"You hungry my nigga?" He called out from the kitchen.

"Nah, nigga I can't even think about food right now," I replied still thinking of all the other events going on in my life at the moment.

Moments later Rock emerged from the kitchen with a plate in his hand that he held close to his face as he shoved forkfuls of food in his mouth.

"So, what's going on nigga? Why you sound like the feds were after you on the phone?" He asked sarcastically.

"I just found out Bianca was pregnant," I replied sitting down on the couch.

"Damn nigga, that's why I don't take bitches to hotel rooms for Valentine's Day," he laughed, with a mouth full of food.

I mean I was upset that he was laughing because this shit was serious to me, even though his words rang true. Two weeks earlier, I was in a completely different place in my life, then boom! Valentine's Day happens.

"Man, this shit is real-life man. I'm 17 years-old my nigga. I dropped out of high school; the job I have is shit and now I have a fucking baby on the way," I snapped as reality fell on me hard.

"Calm down nigga, it's just a baby. Ant, you like my fucking brother. I would never have you out here fucked up nigga. As long as my pockets laid so are yours," Rock replied finishing up his food and taking his plate in the kitchen.

"Man, I don't think that dope life is for me though," I replied finally voicing my insecurities.

"Nigga it is other ways for you to make money, but I will give you money and help you get on yo feet," He replied, coming out of the kitchen and flopping down on the couch.

"I'm listening, nigga." I was now interested in what he had to say.

"You ever shot a nigga?" He asked with a straight face.

"Nah, I ain't never did shit like that," I was now curious to where he was going with the conversation.

"Okay, look. I will find you something. For right now, take this." He tossed me a stack of money with three rubber bands wrapped around it.

"Rock, talk to me man!" I snapped, peeping his change in subject.

"Iight, so the muthafucka I work for has me on a team called The Cleaners. Basically, what I do is when niggas owe him money and they start dodging him or showing signs that they don't want to pay, he sends me out to either get money or bring back their head." He spoke like everything he was saying was normal.

"They pay you, right?" I asked, getting more and more interested.

"Hell yeah, they pay me. Good too," Rock chuckled.

"You think I could do it?" I asked, trusting his judgment.

"Nah, you ain't a killa at heart, but I'm sure I could find you something to do. Until I do though, I will keep you and your family afloat." Rock walked over to me and reaching his hand out to dap me up.

I dapped him up and thanked him, shoving the stack of money in my pocket before I headed back to the apartment. When I pulled into the projects, everything felt different. It was like what was okay for me growing up wasn't okay for my child growing up. I knew that anything I did with Rock could get me killed, but I also knew that there were no nine-to-fives out there that would give me the kind of money that I needed at this moment.

I parked the truck and got out, making a beeline for the apartment. When I walked in Bianca was laying on the couch, snuggled in the covers watching tv.

"Hey baby," She cooed when she saw me.

"Hey. How are you feeling? Did you get some rest?" I asked trying to bring my adrenaline down.

"Are you okay?" She asked, rubbing my face.

"I'm good, you good right?" I asked for reassurance.

"I'm good," she replied, kissing me on the forehead.

I laid back on the couch as she wrapped her arms around me. Closing my eyes, I tried to get my life to slow down for just a second.

# ALEX

Shay had been in the house with me and Kalel for about two weeks now and shit was going good. Kalel was able to get her in the clubs because she was 18, so she was bringing in a steady income. I was still doing parties to make money. I had been thinking about what Remi told me when I talked to her, but I didn't know what to do. All of it could be set up and at this point, I wasn't for anybody's shit. My plan was to take my money and get the fuck out of here.

Kalel was much nicer than normal lately. I couldn't tell if it was because he was fucking Shay or because she was bringing in so much money. Hell, I chalked it up to both. I didn't give a fuck either way. Now he was someone else's headache, no harm no foul. However, I had graduated from weed blunts laced with cocaine to straight cocaine. I had started to lose weight and my hair was starting to fall out. The crazy part was I was hungry as fuck and I could eat my weight, it just wouldn't stay.

I was sleeping all the time and when I was awake, I was walking around with a banging ass headache of my own. At first, I thought I was coming down with something, but then I noticed that I hadn't had my period. I was sitting on the toilet trying to remember the last time I had one. I pulled my phone out of my pocket and opened my period app on my phone. It showed that I, in fact, had not had a period and was working on not having a second one.

I stuffed my phone back in my pocket and wiped, damn near jumping off of the toilet pulling my pants up. I went back into the bedroom to wake Kalel up.

"Kalel, wake up," I said shaking him from his slumber.

"What...what's up, Alex," he replied groggily without opening his eyes.

"I need you to get up for real," I replied shaking him harder.

He finally popped up with an attitude.

"What is it!" He snapped snatching the cover from me.

"I'm pregnant!" I shouted, getting tired of going round and round with him.

"Pregnant?" He asked confused, waking right on up.

"That's what I said," I snapped at him, starting to get irritated.

"Who's the daddy?" He laid back down.

I was crushed. I wanted to be mad at him so bad for the words that had just come out of his mouth. He knew I couldn't and so did I because of the events that had taken place. I sat there with my mouth hanging open, looking for something to rebuttal with, but I had nothing.

"I don't know," I said in almost a whisper.

"What?" He shouted loudly.

"I don't know who the daddy is, okay," I spat at him, starting to cry at the reality of my own words.

"Thot box ass bitch," He spat, chuckling as he rolled over.

I don't know what came over me, but I jumped on top of him and just started hitting him where ever my punches landed.

"Get the fuck off me, you crazy ass bitch!" He shouted throwing me off of him and onto the floor.

He jumped on top of me and started slapping me in the face over and over. He grabbed my hair, banging my head into the floor.

"Let me go!" I finally got the strength to scream out.

"You trying to die, bitch!" He screamed in my face still gripping my hair.

"Kalel, please let me go!" I cried out, fearing for my life after seeing the evil in his eyes.

"I been trying to be nice to your dumb ass, but you keep trying me," he screamed, spit flying all over my face.

"Let's just talk about this," I cried out looking up and seeing Shay standing in the doorway of the bedroom. I assumed we woke her up with our tussling.

"Keep your fucking hands off of me, you understand! You touch me again and I will kill you," Kalel snapped, finally letting me go.

He got up, pushing me off of him and walking towards Shay. She backed up, scared that she was next. He fumbled around the bathroom for a minute then he stormed out of the front door. Shay rushed over to me, helping me up on the bed.

"Oh my god, Alex are you okay?" She asked with sheer concern in her face.

"I'm fine." I wiped the blood from my top lip that had run down from my nose.

"Hold on, I'll get you some tissue." Shay rushed to the bathroom and quickly returned with the tissue.

"Thank you," I replied taking the tissue from her and wiping my nose.

Shay sat down at the end of the bed. "How long has he been putting his hands on you like this?"

"He's only done it a few times." I listened to how dumb the words sounded coming out of my mouth.

"Why do you stick around for this?" She asked.

"I don't have anywhere to go," I lied, not wanting to tell her my plans.

"I hope I don't have to ever go through that," she said, not really knowing what else to say. I mean it wasn't anything that she could do to change it.

"It's cool, I got it under control," I replied, laying back on the bed hoping that my nose would stop bleeding.

I urged her to continue on with her day and get ready for her shift. Kalel had her on 12-hour shifts and I didn't want her day to end up like mine. Plus, I wanted to be alone. I was embarrassed enough already. Forty-five minutes later, the apartment was silent, and I was all alone. I broke down as soon as I heard the door close. I was pregnant. I had no idea who the father of my baby was, and the guy that I was supposed to be with treated me like a piece of property.

I grabbed my phone and called Remi.

"Hey Alex, everything okay?" she asked as if she knew why I was calling.

"Can you come and get me please?" I said breaking down on the phone.

"Send me the address. I'm on my way," She replied and then ended the call.

I sent her the address and found some clothes to wear. I didn't even care to pack, I just wanted to leave. I went in the closet and found the shoebox that I had hidden in the corner with my money in it and stuffed it all in my purse. I opened up my text messages and shot Anthony a text message.

> **Me**: *Hey, I know you probably don't want to hear from me, I know you and Bianca are a thing now I just really need someone I can trust to talk to. Call me if you can.*

I stuck my phone in my back pocket and walked out of the apartment. Remi must not have been far from me because she was pulling up just as I walked out of the door. I got in the car and put my seatbelt on. Remi looked at all my battle scars from my recent scuffle.

"What happened?" She asked pulling off.

"I'm pregnant," I blurted out. It didn't make sense to prolong it.

"What…oh my god, what are you going to do?" she asked in a panicked tone.

"What do you mean what am I going to do?" I asked.

"Are you going to keep it?" She glanced at me and then back at the road.

"Not if I don't have to, I don't even know who the father is, Remi!" I snapped. I was devastated that my life had turned out this way.

Remi didn't say anything for a while, she just stared ahead at traffic. I sat back in my seat, looking out the window thinking about my next step.

"Alex, I am so sorry you have to go through this,"

Remi said finally breaking the silence.

"Yeah, me too," I replied sarcastically still looking out of the window.

My phone buzzed in my pocket I grabbed it and opened the notification. I saw that Anthony had replied to my text.

*Anthony: I will call you in a second.*

I closed the message and waited for his call. A few minutes later, my phone started to ring.

"Hello." I said hesitantly, knowing who it was.

"Hey, everything okay?" Anthony's voice came through the phone like silk.

"Not really," I replied, breaking down instantly hearing his voice.

"What's up… talk to me," Anthony's voice dripped with concern.

"I'm pregnant Anthony, I don't know who the father is because Kalel sold me to some of his friends and it could be any one of them," I replied, sobbing softly.

"Oh damn, that's fucked up Alex. Where are you now?" He asked. I could hear the worry in his voice.

"I'm safe. Do you think maybe we could talk face to face? There is some shit that I think needs to be set straight," I replied, telling him just enough to stop the questions. I didn't want him too involved in my bullshit. I just needed a real friend that I could trust.

"Okay look, I have to take Bianca to the doctor. I will call you when I get back," he said, waiting for me to reply.

"The doctor?" I asked before I thought about it.

"Yeah, they just wanna check on the baby," he said casually.

"The baby?" I repeated, trying to catch my breath.

"Yeah. Look, we will talk, but I have to go now."

"Okay call me back," I hung up the phone.

It felt like everything around me was crumbling. My life was all fucked up and then I find out that Anthony is having a baby with Bianca and he said it like he didn't even care. I laid my head back as the hot tears began to run down my face. At this point, nothing was going right, and it looked like I was stuck in the shit.

"You okay?" Remi asked, reminding me that she was even there.

"I guess," I said dryly.

"What's up?" She asked pulling up to the house that I had seen her in last.

"Nothing I want to talk about Rem," I spat at her.

"Well, you know I am here when you're ready." She parked the car and got out.

I got out of the car behind her and followed her into

the house.

"You can take a hot shower. The closet is full of stuff; I'm sure you can find something in your size." Remi walked towards the back house and returned with a rag and towel for me.

"Thank you Remi," I said, taking the towel and rag from her.

"No worries, I am just glad that you got away from that crazy ass nigga. I will call the clinic and make you an appointment if you want," She replied waiting for my response.

"That would be good thanks," I replied quickly walking way before the tears started again.

I went down the stairs and into the basement. I looked around to get familiar with the layout of everything. My phone started to ring again. I looked down at it and saw that it was Kalel. My heart started pounding; I was terrified that he would know where I was and come straight to me. I sat my phone down on the couch and waited for it to stop ringing. When it finally stopped I was able to breathe again. I grabbed the towel and rag that Remi had given me and went in search of the bathroom.

I was amazed at how they had the basement really set up like a one-bedroom apartment. It was homey and comfy as well, I felt like I was safe. I finished my shower and wrapped the towel around me while walking into the bedroom and opening the closet. Remi had said that the closet was full, but I had no idea it was from wall to wall, floor to ceiling.

I finally figured out something to wear and headed back to the area with the bar. Remi was already sitting on the couch with her drink in her hand. She had poured me one as well that she had sat on the table. She started talking before I even made it to the couch.

"So, you have an appointment tomorrow morning."

"Thanks, Rem," I replied, hanging my head.

"I know this is hard. I have been here before, but it's for the best. You don't want this kind of shit hanging over your head," she said in a calm, understanding tone.

"I hear you, but that doesn't make me feel any better," I replied taking a sip of my drink, wincing as it went down burning my chest on the way.

"I get it, but after tomorrow you have a clean slate to do better." She rubbed my hand.

"I guess you're right," I replied.

I jumped when I heard the loud footsteps above our heads. I just knew that Kalel had found me. Remi jumped up from the couch, headed to see what was going on upstairs. I heard the footsteps stop and her talking. I heard a voice I didn't know and then I heard a voice that was very much so familiar.

I got up from the couch and started to creep up the stairs. When I came around the corner I broke down. Anthony stood there looking at me like he hadn't seen me in years. He rushed over to me scooping up in his arms.

"Alex, I am so glad that you are okay," He whispered in my ear.

"I'm trying, I am glad to see you," I replied not really knowing what to say.

"So, now that ya'll have had ya'll moment, it's time to get down to business," Remi said snatching us from our moment.

She headed back down in the basement and Anthony, the other guy that he was with and I followed behind her. I couldn't believe that I was looking at Anthony in the flesh. I thought that I would never see him again. What really mattered the most was the fact that I finally felt safe now that he was here. Remi cut straight to the point once we were all in the basement.

"Rock, what the fuck is going and who the fuck is this?" She spat at the guy that Anthony was with.

"This my cousin Anthony on my daddy's side. I need to find him a job," Rock replied with a hopeful look on his face.

"What does that have to do with me?" Remi asked. I could see the irritation building in her face.

"I know you need somebody to keep an eye on Alex and I figured Ant here would be the best person for the job," Rock replied looking over and Anthony.

"Alex, how do you feel about that?" Remi asked looking over at me.

"Its fine by me," I replied looking at Anthony.

It was crazy what being away from someone for just a small amount of time could do to their appearance. Anthony was looking like a whole new man and it was nice on him. I was feeling the whole bodyguard thing. It was like something inside of him had switched and he had tapped into his savage. He wasn't wearing that cute little soft side anymore.

The nigga had my box on ten I couldn't even lie, I thought back to all the times I tried to tell myself I didn't like him, finally telling myself that was a lie. I had to hurry and look away when I noticed that he was about to look my way. I could tell there was something on his mind as well, but I knew that eventually, we would get the chance to talk since he is keeping an eye on me and all.

"So, what's the plan with Kalel?" Remi asked looking over at Rock.

"Two days and that bitch is good as gone," Rock

replied with pure malice in his voice.

"Where are we putting Alex until then?" Anthony asked with concern in his tone.

"Did you have somewhere in mind?" Rock asked, looking over at him.

"She can go back to the apartment with me," Anthony replied without hesitation.

"You cool with that?" Rock asked, looking over at me.

"Yeah," I said, almost too fast.

So, the plan was set. I was going back to the projects with Anthony, which wasn't a bad plan for real because Kalel wouldn't think to look for me there first. In his mind, I had no reason to go back there. I couldn't lie, I was scared as hell because I didn't want anything to happen to Anthony or myself for that matter. I grabbed my shit and followed Anthony to his truck.

We didn't say much to each other at first, but once we got rolling, Anthony finally broke the silence.

"How have you been?" He asked as he scanned the radio for something to listen to.

"Miserable, honestly," I replied as honestly as I could.

"Talk to me." His voice was doing something to me.

"I am addicted to cocaine, my boyfriend sold me to

some of his friends for $500 and now I'm pregnant and don't know who the father of my child is," I blurted out, glad to get everything off my chest and know that I wouldn't be judged for it.

"Do you want to stop?" He asked glancing over at me.

"What?...I mean yeah, sometimes, but other times the thought of stopping scares me. It's just too much going on in my life for me to do it sober," I replied feeling like a piece of shit.

"I will help you stop if you want.".

"That would be dope I guess, thanks, Anthony. So, are you really having a baby with Bianca?" I asked.

"Yeah, I am," he replied with a remorseful tone.

"How did that happen? You didn't even like her?" I was trying not to sound too angry.

"When I found out you were with Kalel, at first, I was shocked, but when you stopped coming around and it settled in that you were really fucking with that bum ass nigga, I was fucked up. I mean I had mad feelings for you, and you shitted on me, so I moved on. Bianca came around right after your boyfriend shot me and I was vulnerable. She knew what to say and do at the right time. One thing lead to another and now we are having a baby." I thought I could hear a little unhappiness in his words, but I wasn't one to pry.

"Well at least you weren't putting your hands on her," I replied sarcastically.

"You know I would never put my hands on a woman. My father would get up out of his grave and beat my ass," Anthony replied chuckling.

I chuckled slightly as well, thinking back on my encounters with Kalel. We finally pulled into the parking lot of the projects. My stomach started to turn as all the memories I had, good and bad, played back in my head.

"You good?" Anthony asked parking the truck and looking over at me.

"Yeah, it's just a lot of memories that's all," I replied exhaling slowly.

"I can understand that," He replied getting out of the truck.

I got out of the truck as well catching up to him as he walked up on the sidewalk. When we walked into the apartment I started to get a weird feeling. I sat down in the reclining chair closest to the door.

"Baby, you're finally back," I heard a female voice say as Anthony walked into the dining room.

When Bianca came around the corner and saw me sitting there I could have sworn I saw steam come out of her ears she was so pissed.

"What the fuck is this bitch doing here!" She shouted, walking into the living room between me and Anthony.

"We can talk about it later," Anthony replied, trying to diffuse the bomb that was waiting to explode.

"Who the fuck you calling a bitch?" I spat at her. After all the shit that I had been through, I was waiting to take it out on someone.

"I'm talking to you, thot ass bitch!" She shouted, not giving a fuck about what Anthony was talking about.

"Bitch fuck you! Rachet ass hood rat," I snapped at her.

She pushed Anthony out of the way trying to get to me. I stood up ready for whatever she wanted to do.

"You better learn your place bitch," Bianca spat at me over Anthony's arms since he was now standing between us.

"Girl fuck you!" I shouted at her, sitting back down in the chair once I saw she wasn't about that life.

"Everybody calm the fuck down! Shit! I don't have time for this bullshit!" Anthony shouted at both of us.

In the midst of all the drama, there was a knock at the door stopping all three of us in our tracks. Anthony walked over to the window and looked out. He walked over to the door and opened it. Remi stepped into the apartment with her gun in her hand and a deep frown on her face. Rock was following close behind her.

"Rock, what the fuck is going on?" Anthony asked in a panic, his adrenaline already pumping.

Remi and Rock walked quietly to the couch and sat down before Remi started to talk.

"Now as everyone in this room knows, Rock is my baby brother, the only brother I have, actually. So, when I find out that someone is trying to set him up, you can see how that would upset me. It's even more upsetting to find out that the reason my brother is being set up is to get to someone else in his circle, which would mean that it would be someone in my family as well." She paused and looked around the room, then directly at Bianca.

When I looked over at Bianca, she looked like she had seen a ghost. I was starting to put two and two together, but I wanted to hear what else Remi had to say. The room grew eerily quiet as Remi continued.

"So, Bianca, do you want me to tell Anthony how you and Kalel are scheming a plot for Kalel to get revenge on Rock out of jealously? Or how you tried tapping him with this baby to keep Alex under Kalel's thumb, out of another plot formed from your hate of Alex?" Remi asked looking over at Bianca who was now wringing her hands together.

"I trapped him, so what! Alex didn't deserve him, and it was easy. He is weak as fuck when it comes to Alex and when she left, that was the perfect opportunity for me to shoot my shot. That bitch always had everything and I never had anything! I used to watch the way that he would cater to her and she would blow him off like he was nothing. Then there I was throwing myself at him and I got nothing!"

Before anyone could say anything, Anthony lunged at Bianca.

"You bitch!" He shouted, grabbing her up by the collar, pushing her into the wall and wrapping his hands around her throat.

Rock jumped up trying to get Anthony off of Bianca, I could understand his pain, but I had never seen him like that before.

"I knew this shit was too good to be true you spiteful ass bitch, I will fucking kill you, bro! stop fucking with me!" Anthony shouted.

Rock finally got Anthony off of Bianca, as she slid down the wall trying to catch her breath. I sat there trying to register everything that was going on before me. I was stuck on the fact that the whole time that had been getting my body sold and being treated like a sack of shit she was behind it out of revenge. Her and Kalel had been playing role hard as shit. I don't know where it came from but something in me triggered my crazy and before I knew it I jumped up and started swinging on Bianca.

Everyone rushed over to get us apart then out of nowhere

*Bang Bang!*

Two shots rang out and everything after that was a blur.

# TO BE CONTINUED

*Don't forget to follow me:*

*Instagram: Shewritesbooks28*

*Facebook: @TheRealJenee*

*For all Updates & New Releases*

CPSIA information can be obtained
at www.ICGtesting.com
Printed in the USA
LVHW041949061120
670968LV00003B/384